C000137063

SELFIE, SUICIDE

or Cairey Turnbull's Blue Skiddoo

By Logo Daedalus

For my most outstanding loans.

"The water of the forest is still & felicitous
& we, we can be vicious & full of pain."
-Nils Runeberg

INCOMPREHENSIBLE FRAGMENT

...the nameless knight in Lucremorn
by sorcerer accursed
awaited for unending days
his muse's fate's reverse
by reddened signs of sacrifice,
the toll that was foretold,
when on a brisk & moonlit night
with an unearthly cold
he'd sailed for the remotest isle
by vessel that he'd stole
above the satyrs' labyrinth
to resurrect her soul.
He faced the fire breathing snake,
by grace of Lucremorn.
He sought the way of recompense
& mending what had torn.
Somewhere the star of death's redress
was hid within the deeps
where mortal eyes had never crept
nor mortal fingers reached.
"It is not lost & can be found"
began the dragon's speech
"but this alone is not a cause
for mortal hope's relief
as men far braver than yourself
have sought for it in vain
unable to afford its cost,
a lifetime spent in pain...
You must drift in Lucremorn
until the sky's ablaze
& blood from other realms is paid-
& then, she'll leave the maze..."

THE ENTRANCE

Cairey Turnbull is precariously perched on the edge of a fall. His head is heavy & half-floating. He's buzzing with thoughts like the sun-sagged balloons that litter the bedroom of his tenement. His musings are unballasted. They sway in the invisible shifts & drafts of any wind's decree. He's buzzing & bubbling under the influence of bottomless brunch mimosas, & he's swaying aimlessly, but swaying safely still. He's been able to avoid an alluring slip into the shallows of intoxication. For now, there's a residual fortification in his guts- an eggs benedict, half digested, still maintains its salubrious sponginess as it floats upon a hollandaise foam beside a flotsam of duck bacon bobbing beside it like the remains of a shipwreck in the maelstrom of his digestion.

He's holding a door aloft. His shadow has already entered the foyeur of the Museum of Expressive Humanism, but his body remains, hanging from its door, as he's misjudged the heft of this delusively transparent entryway, & in his struggle to pull it open against the force of the street-sweeping gale, a loose strand of his overcoat hooked itself onto its handle. After forcing the door & losing his balance as the wind's force shifted in his favor, he discovers that he has become ensnared. This is how we find Cairey Turnbull, our most lamentable specimen.

Hanging over a puddle which reflects the overcast sky, warped by the warring circumferences of sporadic stillicides, he feels, once again, a sensation which reflects the eeriness of his station. He's haunted by his life's regrets. He feels a presentiment, again, of that horrific revelation, the one which taunts his waking hours announcing his damnation. This dreadful ambience is amplified by mist & haze from the dribbling incessance of this late-morning rain, which renders his surroundings as obscured as his hopes, & weighs on his shoulders like his moist winter coat.

He hadn't slept well, but he rarely slept unmolested by bad dreams. He had greeted his alarm with the panic of an overdue lateness, as it had interrupted a phantom of his adolescent anxieties in the guise of a guidance counselor, as it so often was, as she was informing him that he'd missed every deadline, appointment, & test, & was consequently doomed to his woes, distresses, & of course, his regrets...

So he's drowsy and out of sorts, but he's been that way for years. This thought is itself routine, & if he were honest, it doesn't come to him without a hint of vertiginous thrill. He's addicted to the sensation of being on the brink & he's enchanted with the visions of ego-squashing ecstasy that accompany it. His botched quests for revelations, mystifications, purposes, always lead him to appels du vide- a phrase that he has enjoyed rolling around his mouth like a hard candy ever since learning it in one of his youniversity courses, enjoying the polyglottic resemblance that Dr. McTeuf had pointed out, to those doubly forbidden apples of eternal life, which in the Garden of Hesperides... well, Cairey never swallowed them whole- these original choking hazards, these myths...

No, Cairey is not a brave boy. He's always shirked his readings & his duties. Truly, he only enjoys the flirtation with these dangerous ideas- delighting in the gnaw & dance & shuffling along the edge of a plunge which seems so tantalizing, but never... He chocks it up today to the chemicals in his bloodstream- the caffeine from his morning draught of cold-coffee, the side-effects of his prescription pills, the fetid soup of his abnormal brain, & of course, all of that uncelebratory champagne he'd quaffed in citric disguise. All of these poisons combined so early in the AM explain his lack of poise or so he assures himself. The nauseous sensation in his throat is tied in his mind to a sort of car-sickness he suffers from which emerges as soon as he begins to walk after sitting so long in transit that the sudden expansion of space from hermetic enclosure & the resultant blood rush to his semi-sleeping limbs spurs a lightheadedness & a blind dizziness which makes the ablest of surfaces feel as trepidatious as standing alone in an unwieldy canoe.

Needless to say, Cairey's warped & unbalanced, & more-than-figuratively hanging from a thread. The simian sturdiness of upright normalcy is just beyond his grasp. All he has are his instincts & anxieties from which he hangs by his sleeve- & neither of these are heralded as reliable navigators of the vast unmapped & the mysterious phatic unspoken.

But as he's hanging from the door to the Museum of Expressive Humanism, he allows, with accidental chivalry, his algorithmically assigned date to pass before him. This provides him the opportunity to inspect her posterior anatomy with a libidinal flick of his hazel eyes. So far he's lacked this vantage on her & he's something of an expert in judging the three-dimensional curves rendered by the nude female form. He believes he can see through clothes, given the proper vantage. Up to now, he's only known her as a two-dimensional figurette- a carefully curated avatar, a hint younger, & more than a clue slimmer, with a name he'd learned to be a pseudonym devised by her roommate to "keep the creeps at bay"- & so far, she's done nothing to complicate these first impressions & disappointments, nor has she provided any authentic scaffold to replace it. All of her outer significances are easily mapped to a type Cairey has an unwilling attraction to, despite the fact that he's sworn off this- as he has thought- "feminine junkfood."

Her hair is dark at its roots, but the bulk of it is bleached blonde & tipped with a chemical pink- like a neapolitan fudgsicle, the sort with a strawberry that tastes of bubblegum, a watery yellowed vanilla honed to cut manufacturing costs, & a chocolate that only melts on your fingers, dripping down the balsa wood grip & staining your hands with a henna tattoo of asymmetrical insignificance. Her eyes are brown & framed by a raccoon smudge of eyeliner, tapered to a triangular flourish- like the wings of horus. Beneath her coat she wears a baggy turtleneck which hangs like a pastel pink hospital gown over a pair of baggy sunbleached momjeans. The combination renders all physique below her neck utterly imperceptible. She is opaque. It's a style all the rage these days amongst fretfully aging twenty-somethings. She's normal, he thinks.

& so Cairey, still hanging from the door, but having finally circumnavigated his date, finds here nothing but another bottomlessness, another surface revealing nothing underneath. & it is now with the death of his erotic hopes for a satisfying engagement with normalcy that his general unresponsiveness takes on the funereal tenor of mourning. He cannot find the limits of his regrets- from setting out on today's abysmal venture to the abysmal venture of his birth.

He'd had another dream the night before. He was on the top floor of a skyscraper, with a thunderstorm looming over the city. It was raining so heavily that the streets below were lost in a mist. The only lights were from parallel skyscrapers reflecting the lightning which forked & shattered the clouds. Thunder cracked like a felled tree & boomed like the impact of its fall. He had been alone in his dream. He was in a skyline bar with rotating floors. It had been stationary at the time as the building had lost power. He had known all of this instantaneously, as one does in dreams, & he'd also known, just as instantaneously, what his dream had destined him to do. His dreams always imposed this sense of inevitability. & so in his dream he ran as fast as he could & burst through the plate glass windows of the skyline bar- falling shards tinkling melodically as they twinkled with reflected lightning- all so slowly, so serenely... It was only as he looked below him & saw the streets demystified, revealing an immense body of water below, that the tug of gravity pulled his projected arc into a parabolic fall. & before he could hit the water, he exploded into a cloud of blood.

He woke to a timpani roll of distant thunder & the hiss of rain on the roof of his tenement. The clock read 4am. His heart was racing. He went back to sleep.

& still hanging there, from the entryway, he thinks of this. He often wishes for such a cinematic ending to his life, & barring that, he'd accept a midseries cancellation ordered by a power beyond his station- or at the very least, an indefinite hiatus without the possibility of a fan clamoured reboot. He wishes for the death of himself or his Director. & this is what he's thinking about as he attempts to liberate himself from the thread tying him to the handle of the door. & these thoughts spur more thoughts, until he finds himself unspooling his associative web to the source of this idea- something his date had said over their exhaustive brunch.

After an introduction pained with confusion over the proper gesture of greeting- his extended handshake denied for an awkward one-armed shoulder hug- & after an eternity of uncomfortable silence during which they perused the brunch menu, they'd spent the majority of their pre-meal anticipation discussing the season finale of a television serial, as well as the critical thinkpieces that trailed in its wake. The subject had been suggested, quite successfully, by the dating platform they had used to meet each other. It was only natural that this- being, apparently, the common ground upon which the seeds of potential affection might flourish into lifelong romance, would appear so early in their algorithmically ordained love story.

The show was called Symon.

Its plot revolved around the insurrectionary & pranksterish exploits of the psuedoeponymous artist-cum-anarchist-cum-cult leader & his disciples. He was portrayed as one of the archtypically cliched antiheroes which are so popular in the medium of serialized televisual drama. & in this sense, the show was not substantially unique. It was one of the many other television serials which strutted the stage of social media relevance, fretting not so much the tossed tomatoes of amateur film critics so much as losing the attention they had garnered. Generally, the goal for such shows was to go out on high, or better, gloriously early, in order to maintain mystique & discussions of "what could have been." Better that than to go woefully late, like so many ill-fated serials, whose finales felt like ill-attended hospital deaths, in which the few remaining mourners pilloried the damn crone with questions about "justice" & "responsibility" & "betrayal of expectations."

As Symon was an antihero, it was obvious to most viewers, by subconscious mythopoetical logic, that his Faustian debt would be repaid in blood in this finale. The transgression that would be punished by this resolution was Symon's implied communions with the occulted terrain of the viewer's world-the realm beyond the screen. This theme was particularly appealing to Cairey, not only for his ineffable aesthetic biases, but because the show was filmed in the very city in which he had lived for far too many years- & of course, it is this same city which so charitably houses the Museum of Expressive Humanism. Symon's city was an alternate take on Cairey's city, with its timeline running parallel to its, albeit, with a slight delay due to the contingencies of production. The show had often dealt with "real" events, & "real" persons- ripping them from the headlines as it were & only barely disguising their inspirations behind flimsily devised parallel names that even the most dull-headed viewer could match to their sources. Even still, there were so many articles spelling out these allusions that it made one wonder...

Symon himself was not an unknown personage in Cairey's world. His name was, in reality, Simon LaFeint, & he was the bohemian son of a wealthy financial lineage. He used his endless personal fortune to fund the show. Little was known about Simon outside of his show. His youth had been spent drifting about the globe, enjoying lavish luxury, & throwing parties that many remembered, though few remembered him personally. He was notoriously difficult to track down, & his few interviews, many suspected, had been composed by himself. They were factually contradictory, otherwise improbable, & generally outlandish. The only solid information to go on came from the public business records of The LaFeint Foundation. It was these interests that obsessed Symon's critical community.

For instance, in the third season of Symon, the city's formerly beloved golden boy Louis Derozio, a now disgraced exile, but then an upstart mayorial candidate, had his extramarital exploits mocked so mercilessly by Symon that the show was often blamed for his electoral humiliation. Derozio's interests in fighting the "elitist intellectuals" of the city's financial lineages put him at odds with the LaFeint family as he had named them in particular. His reputation was destroyed by his parody in the figure "Lewis Deruzual," the antagonist of the season, who was depicted as a hypocritically bigoted "man of the people" & "man of God" who happened to partake in those two most beloved pastimes of upstart politicians- extramarital liaisons with the fourth estate & underaged interns.

The show had delved into stranger territory than that over the years. There were plotlines in which neglected historical & political figures, typically of radical persuasions, were resurrected

& had their grievances aired in lengthy monologues. There were psychedelic episodes in which the city was plagued by the ghosts of the savage Native American tribes who had once hunted on its lands. There was even a one-off episode in the fifth season in which a kaiju composed of the city's sewage fought a mecha personification of its crumbling infrastructure.

Over the years the show had become downright unhinged & difficult to follow, to the delight of its core demographic, the pretentious, overeducated encyclopedists of pop-cultural allusion & contemporary flotsam, like Cairey, & the show's cinematographer. However, in the show's finale, these quirks had exploded beyond the wider audience's expectations. In its final scene, Symon had produced a poster advertisement for the show's final season, familiar to inhabitants of Cairey's city from its ubiquity on subway platforms, bus stops, & the few, somehow still remaining carcasses of phone booths. It asked "IS THIS THE END OF SYMON?" above the trademarked Symon mask, a horned visage carved with an abnormally wide & almost malicious smile, sticking out its tongue, in the style of hellenic comedy masks.

With this poster in hand, Symon revealed to his disciples, a crowd gathered below his perch on top of a tenement cornice, that he was, indeed, the protagonist of this television serial, & worse, that he was a self-insert modeled on the personality of the lead-actor-writer-producer-director, Simon LaFeint- a man with a rather "problematic ego" as the piece-thinkers were so fond of saying. This had been unsurprising as this had been obvious to everyone who watched Symon. What was worse was that he had announced that the "show" was indeed over, & that he'd be leading his gathered disciples- here, speaking directly into the camera with his iconic green eyes spiking its lens- out of their phoney artificial reality in a revolutionary invasion of the desultory realm beyond the screen. He went on to soliloquize about the insufficiency of the medium that his character was embedded in. He claimed that with his talents he would instead reform the World. He said that if he succeeded in his aims, such distractions, like his television serial. would no longer be necessary, as Life-itself would emerge as Art, naturally, from the collected wills of his followers, directed by his unparalleled genius. He asked "Are you with me?" & then the show cut to black.

The proverbial shark had been jumped, as many more than one astute commentator had noted in review. More generally, the wider audience's sympathy had waned with the waxing of the seasons, & this overwhelmingly heavy-handed fourth-wall-breaking meta-shenanigan had missed its mark. What had aimed so loftily at an inspirational & conceptual awe had landed squarely off the target & into the corkboard of "pretension" & "condescension"- far from the critical bullseye of its second season finale, which concurrently rests at 97% on most review- aggregating sites. This had been, critically, the height of Symon. It had been his pop cultural apotheosis, introducing this cult & critical darling into the mainstream. This episode had been seemingly beloved by all, so much so that its climactic scene had become a cultural icon- an orgy of five thousand disciples mounting each other in a farcical pornographic display in the center of LaFeint Park. Symon sermonized from a megaphone on the Liberation of all Libidinal Desires as the ultimate aim of enlightened humanity. Was this only the pride before the fall? Was this episode's title "Symon's Complete Hubris" much less ironical now, in retrospect? Such were the questions asked by reviewers in their headlines & answered in the very act of their asking. Was this sort of "postmodern play & parody" really so revolutionary after all?

Something had changed. It was quantifiable. The finale had been so harshly panned that even this formerly adored image had become the subject of ridicule for the commentariat- even those vultures of dead trends, the late-night standup pundits, had made monologue fodder of it. The few early-adopting

Symon-contrarians were riding victory laps, waving their banners of "I Told You So" before the crowd of viewers who had decided, finally, that they were not with Symon after all.

"It was groan-inducing"- is what Cairey's date had said, with a confidence bolstered by the critical consensus. She pointed at the 33% aggregate rating she'd pulled up on her phone, all- the-while unaware of a verdant distraction crooked by her incisor. "I wish they'd just killed him off like everyone thought they would. That would have wrapped it up nicely. Cliffhanger-endings like this are just like- ugh. Like what, is he setting up for a movie or something? Is he gonna like, run for President? I'm still annoyed at it." To this Cairey had nodded, nearly grimacing as she swiped that vestigial bit of vegetation with her critical tongue- an image now linked in his mind to the windshield wiper he'd watched on their ride to the museum from brunch.

It had hypnotized him. His eyes followed its pendulous motion- back-and-forth- as it snagged a rain soaked leaf & waved it in quarter-circle arcs. He had been nearly deaf to her incessant deluge of syllables- about the show, about the buildings they passed, the streets, the cars, the pedestrians, the brands & billboards & songs & snippets of commercials that emanated from the car's compulsory speakers. To all of it, everything she said, he agreed & nodded rhythmically- down with each returning swipe of the wiper & up with each perpendicular thud.

& with all of this racing through his mind in scattered form, Cairey finally frees his sleeve from the handle of the door by snapping the loose thread with a violent jerk. He nearly bumps into his date, as she has paused in the entryway without entering, exhaling dramatically in a display of reverence, as if before a great Buddha seen after a lifelong pilgrimage, or before any other mecca of ostensible gravity, imbued with the power to grant life's meaning, some revelation, or purpose to render all hardships & sufferings of the trail sublime.

"Don't you just adore the MEH?" she asks. Cairey doesn't share her evident enthusiasm, but does his best to make it out like he does- still nodding as one does when one's mind has wandered off down silent interior corridors.

There's no use arguing with assigned dates, he thinks, especially with a reputation as bad as his own from all of his unfortunate unpleasantnesses, his various fuck-ups as he calls them to his therapist. It has been a long time since his last first date, if that had even counted as a date, & it has only been a year since the day of the breakup of the only relationship he's ever had. That day had been a fuckup so monstrous in proportion that its consequences were carved into his social-credit score, which had dipped into a pit so deep, that he's only recently proved himself barely-acceptable to the algorithms that governed dating-service registrations. It has only been days since he has been able to put himself on the market again, & he is still in the precarious position of "probational approval"- but he isn't thinking about any of this in the soft & padded recesses of his soul, in his secret chamber of silent solemnity.

He's still thinking about Symon. He's thinking about how much he absolutely adores its finale, still, despite all of the criticisms he has ingested. He still admires the show-runner's tricks, his gestures toward & perturbations of this realm beyond the screen. He is amused by each of his spikings of the camera lens. He doesn't understand how it's possible for his judgment to so diverge from the critical consensus, though he knows that there's no use arguing about it, much less defending it on grounds he's unable to formulate. Perhaps, he thinks, he should have mentioned to her that he'd seen them filming that last scene, on that very worst day of his life actually, & that he could be seen in the overhead crowd shot amongst Symon's gathered disciples. Perhaps, he thinks, Symon's rhetorical question meant something much more to him considering he had

15

overheard it unmediated by the show itself, & that this very fact placed him in a privileged position, as, perhaps, a true disciple of Symon's.

Perhaps she would have found that case of synchronic serendipity amusing, at least- or, & more likely, she would have only pretended to, all-the-while being amused, instead, by his attempt to show off- as if encountering a film crew on the streets of their city was anything but a daily occurrence- as if being incidentally on camera was some accomplishment- as if he were some bumbling tourist taking note of the skyscrapers- as if he were amazed by the daily procession of the Sun- as if his life's greatest accomplishment wasn't this pathetic, insignificant inclusion in the margins of another's critical failure.

He still finds it interesting, anyway. He delights in the fact that he hadn't known at the time that this was the scene he'd seen, nor anything about Symon, as he'd only watched its backlog after running into the crew & becoming enamored by the spectacle. Nor had he known then that he had been included in it. Still, he feels that this alone cannot explain why he likes it, as he did like it, even at the time. He likes it even more now that he's seen it through the framing of all of its episodes, & the context of the show as an entirety, even more than can be justified by the mere fact of having been a minor appendage in its production. He guesses that he likes the audacity of the whole thing- perhaps, he thinks, out of his misplaced confidence in the power of Art to escape from its frame of artifice & inspire some change in reality? But what has the show- what has Art ever done for him, really, but distract him, momentarily, from the unending tragedies of his life?

& this question comes to him like a knock on a door. & there, within that internal cell where he has been momentarily safe from destructive analysis, a door is thrown open. His mind's guests are always knocking only to enter unbidden- knocking only to warn of their inevitable entrances. A parade of uninvited thoughts storm in, arms crossed behind their backs, to remind him in a chorus, in voices tinged with benign scorn, that people like what they like- they dislike what they dislike- & only narcissists like himself have the audacity to suggest that their judgments are wrong. They remind him that these un-moored cretins, such as himself, who insist on the superiority of their taste against the critical consensus are only signaling to some fictitious audience their ultimately grandiloquent sense of superiority in culture, which they believe, delusionally, to be synonymous with some sort of virtue. They remind him that such thinking is merely symptomatic of alienated, insecure, & certifiably insane self-obsessive schizotypals whose egos can-not bear the collective truths of the social construction that we like to call reality.

They remind him that this motivated reasoning is deployed as a defense mechanism for grandiose delusions. They remind him of a particular truth, which he knows so well that he often sub-vocalizes it as a mantra & banishing ritual: No one cares, Cairey.

No one has cared or will ever care for the productions of his dis-eased mind- all of these thoughts & opinions & vague gestures at ideas that spew into his consciousness like exhaust fumes into the atmosphere. They're as predictable & pollutive as any consequence of late industrial society. They're the mutilated chirps of birds diseased by factory runoff. & Cairey, over the last year, has become downright fond of reminding himself such things. He feels the burden of his self-conscious analysis lift from his shoulders. He forces a wry smile, & smiling, he takes a step from his introverted cell, & shuts the real door of the real Museum behind him.

"Well?" she asks, as she hangs her coat over his shoulder. He is stripping himself of his overcoat, the one he'd bought at a Goodwill, under the duress of his ever-dwindling finances & the grey cosmopolitan snow. This unexpected encumbrance throws off his instinctual rhythm. "Oh'fcourse" he manages, barely avoiding the certain offense of kissing her coat to the floor. I should listen to her, he reminds himself, she's trying to be amicable with me- despite the fact that I ignored her the whole ride here, just to stare at a fucking leaf. I'm uninteresting. My brain is fucked up. I've bungled every question she's asked me. She must think I'm abnormal. Maybe even deranged. She's probably uncomfortable with me. Fair enough. She'll savage me in review. I'm fucking up again. & I'll deserve it. I deserve worse.

She interrupts his thoughts with an announcement, her eyes scanning the heavens of the vestibule. She says "I haven't been here in forever" with forever enunciated like the name of a prestigious brand, "When was the last time you were here Cairey?" & it is with this deployment of his proper name that Cairey realizes that he's forgotten hers & can only remember the name of her avatar- the name which had attracted him & convinced him to accept the date arrangement in the first place, the name he'd only learned, like so many things in his life, to be fraudulent upon further inspection. He wracks his mind, but can only remember "Abigail Wazir," the name she'd used to shield herself from "creeps & stalkers," but he remembers nothing more than this.

"Uh- years I think. It was years ago. A long time ago."

Unheedful of his thought's council, he is once more thrown into his introverted analysis. He completely ignores her follow-up to his answer to her question- which was only asked, really, as a means of gaining approval to once more, go-on & on & on about herself. So as she's recounting her last Museum excursion, trilling with superlative adjectives & hyperbolic analogies, Cairey drafts a plot to procure her proper name in such a fashion that will not let on that he's procuring it at all.

He's halted in the sketching phase of this plan.

A disquieting shadow is cast upon him- a shadow in the shape of a prison-tatted Albert Einstein wearing 80s era bling- two Flavor-Flav clocks hanging from his neck, iced out, & ticking with relativistically significant distinction. The source of this shadow is a recently commissioned statue titled "Everybody is a Genius" after the old nuclear weisenheimer's famously misattributed quotation. This is also the title of the Museum's current bifurcated exposition- which bears the subtitles "In Life" & "In Death." The statue had been designed by an acquaintance of Cairey's from his youniversity days- but he knows none of these things. What has halted Cairey in his plotting in the entryway is the advertised prices for entrance on the signboard they're approaching.

He had not considered this. He'd maintained, so far, his assumption that the Museum was free- for-all, or at least, free for residents of the city. It had been free for him when he'd last endured it on assignment as an undergrad at the General Arts Youniversity, back when he was a freshman & still majoring in Socio-Hegemonical Interrogation & Theory. The Youniversity no longer exists. It went bankrupt two years prior, though the debts he owes it are not so kind.

The price-list triggers Cairey's ever-present economic anxieties into the full-blown panic of a budget crisis. He weighs the sum he's already expended on their split brunch & is suffocating in worrisome figures- unable to check his dwindling checking account, he wonders if he'll be able to clear it on credit. The specter of an overcharge fee lingers, & he fears surpassing his bank- regimented monthly spending budget- a standard policy for someone with a social-credit score as low as his- & this fear haunts him with a surly grin- which in his mind becomes the dessert cocktail his date had ordered, which was equal in price to his entree-&-endless-mimosa combo.

It glares at him in his mind's eye, with its mochi-spheres impaled on chocolate straws, diagonally askew, granting an air of cockeyed bemusement to its taunting pareidolic face. She hadn't even offered him a sip of it- never mind a chocolate straw, which he ough't've been allotted at least a portion of. It would have been the right thing to do. He had paid for half of it after all. He chokes the collar of her coat as a pittance of revenge- an act governed by a sort of sympathetic magical logic typical of his habitual acts of impotent impudence. He really wanted a goddamn sip, at the very least- though, he reminds himself, he had never asked for one.

& he certainly hadn't asked to return to the Museum of Expressive Humanism, nevermind pay for the privilege. That was entirely her fault. Or perhaps, he thinks, it was partially the dating service's fault. He hadn't asked her if she'd planned the date herself or if she'd picked a precurated plan. Experience advised him that such an inquiry implied a negative judgment with respect to her creativity, spontaneity, agency, etc. All he had done was advertise himself as free for Sunday, & had been informed on Friday that a date could be arranged with an "Abigail Wazir" if he agreed. The details of the arrangement were not supplied then. He'd known neither the itinerary nor the avatar of his date when he had accepted the invitation. He had only seen the name "Abigail Wazir," & suicidally drunk & stoned as he was, & as lonely & miserable as ever he was, he'd sighed a regretful "fuck it" & swiped right solely for his affection for the name Abigail. As soon as the details were divulged on the confirmation page- he realized what a mistake he had made. A cancellation would have sent him below the acceptability threshold again. & he'd wanted to cancel. Oh, how he'd wanted to cancel. He had come up with a litany of excuses to cancel, but he was too afraid to use them. He decided, instead, to let the date serve as at test for himself. If it went poorly, it would confirm his complete uselessness & if it went well... well, he didn't suspect that it would.

So he looks at her beside him as they reach the ticket booth, hoping she can understand the turmoil in his heart by means of telepathy- & maybe return him some semblance of a sign, a glint of an eye, a flash of a smile, even a freckle of recognition- anything that might recompense his sacrifices & assure him of something good to come in life- but all he finds, so close to her now, is a constellation of zits hiding behind a plaster of cover- up & pale foundation, from which connect-the-dot shapes emerge like from the stucco ceilings of his insomnia. A forma- tion emerges distinctly, running from above her right eye & all the way down...

He looks at his feet. He sighs. It's beyond too late. It's far beyond too late. There will be no escape. He cannot flee on any imagin- able account. Not yet. His boots are cemented to his fate.

"Sir?" asks the man behind the ticketbooth as Cairey raptly in- vestigates the knots in his laces.

Maybe... he thinks, impishly.

"One adult-" he says, but is interrupted by her elbow to his ribs & the pinprick of her disgusted eyes. Her glare stabs into his temple like the tip of a falling icicle.

"One moment please, sorry" he says, perhaps too softly for the ticket man to hear.

"I was under the impression that we were splitting" he whispers "we split the brunch & I thought-"

"We didn't split the ride here. I paid for that. Remember?" she says, her voice raising indignantly for the first time, breaking the whisper-pact of public propriety Cairey had presumed he

21

needn't make- "We had a deal, remember? You agreed on our way here. I didn't mean to raise my voice. I'm sorry, but don't you remember? We went over this."

Cairey knows for an absolute & undeniable fact that he had not uttered a single meaningful or legally-binding syllable in the car, unless "Oh wows" & "that's wilds" were evidences of intent. It's not worth it, he thinks. So he hushes & apologizes with an "alright alright I forgot I got it sorry"- & lets her do the talking. He passes his credit card to the ticket man & prays that that the transaction goes through. It does, & he's handed his receipt after their entrance bracelets are wrapped around their wrists.

The total was 20% more than he'd already expended on brunch. Today, in total, he has expended an amount that could cover his groceries for a month. His brain throbs, drunk & numb on submerged antipathy- a feeling somewhere between an icepick lobotomy & an icecream headache. He should have said no, he thinks, as he knows from research as extensive as it is em-barrassing that girls receive quite frequently- more frequently than the most cynical men even imagine- that girls quite fre-quently receive vouchers from ridesharing services allied with various dating platforms as an incentive to schedule using their particular service. They are included in all prefabricated ar-rangements- & this brunch-museum date is one of the most popular precurated plans. In fact, Cairey has read quite a bit about this, more than can be healthy for his mind. He has read the forums where girls congregate to test various strategies aimed at maximizing their dating ROI- & these things are as obsessively charted & calculated as the strategies of the most dedicated of coupon clipping mothers. He's spent more time investigating such things than he cares to admit to himself- & all that he's gleaned from his investigations is an increasingly malevolent suspicion for this supposedly better half of his mis-erable species.

If only that's all he had- his financial woes- the pains of knowing how defenseless he is to getting snaked & sharked & fucked by bankers, financiers, merchants of goods & experiences. He is used to these. But oh- what is worse than his financial im-miseration is that somewhere beneath his dejection & disaffec-tion a part of him still "believes in Love." & if it wasn't for this remnant of innocence, he could have avoided this dating racket entirely. He loathed this industry of Love with all of its catechisms, its veiled mysteries & rites, now fed into the black box of artificially intelligent management, where Cupid is now computed. & what could Love mean if it meant to fall for the dictates of an unanswerable algorithm, after penances paid- the chic fusion brunch in a gentrifying neighborhood, the encultur-ating museum excursion- these demonstrations of compatible social capitals- perhaps, even, an obligatory gift-shop trinket, & more drinks at some skyline bar... all of these microtransac-tions slicing like lingchi razors, bleeding dollars & decimals in steady faucet drips from a body barely capable of motivating it-self to survive... Was this the end of this Love Business?

Cairey has no authentic answer, save commodifying his loath-somely innate monkey-wishes for penile penitents, for spasms of recognition followed by shame & regret- as if in the wake of any orgasm he'd ever find his fundamental misery & loneli-ness absolved. This comfort had never come. The thought itself disgusts him now. But everything disgusts him now, especially himself.

He'd done the math before. It was a long time ago, before he'd got his first-ever girlfriend. After doing the calculations, he'd sworn off dating in favor of virtual reality pornography. He'd in-vested in a Tinkerbell- that most prestigious brand of synthetic holes, the crown jewel of Sinflate's "Neverland Collection." It saved him hundreds, if not thousands a year by his calculation. He had almost caved again a few months prior. His digital hand hovered over the purchase. He didn't though, as this would have confirmed his eternal loneliness. He still had a small hope of emerging from the brink of normality & staking a claim of the Good Life. He knew the power of these intoxicating fumes. He knew the reprieves of total degeneration. He had lived within their spells for years & had decided, after years of decline, to escape them once & for all or to kill himself & escape them all at once. For a brief period of his life, before he had fucked it all up, he thought he had escaped his misery- but he had only gone south from there.

He knew how simple it could be- should he disabuse himself of this ignoble devotion to Love, whatever that meant anymore. If he considered himself to be no better than a beast with various appetites then how cheaply he could be assuaged- to be a mongrel, to be free... This is what he had thought when he had succumbed to the virtual quellings of all of his desires, only to always find himself at the end of the weekend, at the end of some hedonic bender, feeling the first pang of diminishing returns, alone, & without any further means to assuage his miseries. With a brain fried & devoid of serotonin, he always felt suicidally awful & repentant. He tossed & turned unable to fall asleep or else tormented with bad dreams, promising that he'd straighten up. There were only so many ways he could distract himself from the incorrigible fact of his loneliness before it returned with a vengeance.

It was this dream of escape that had a real hold on him- this notion of Love was only one of its guises. All of these hurdles in the way of his satisfaction were his jailers- bastards- dangling chains of resplendent skeleton keys, promises of freedom & paradise, offering to remove his fetters- for a price, & one he never had the money to pay...

He cannot tell who he thinks is more perverse- these conspiracy conglomerates, these corporate voyeurs in the industries of Love, cheering him on, & laughing at him behind the one-way mirrors of the digital economy- or himself, knowing that their gaze is always upon him, & knowing that they know he knows, & knowing still, performs for them, hoping someday that they free him from his abjection, like a circus chimpanzee.

This is what passes through his mind as they leave the ticket booth. His date retrieves her collapsible selfie-stick from her purse as they pass through the rope-maze gauntlet toward the coat-check. She smiles at it as it extends in her hand. Cairey hands their coats to the coatcheck & receives two tokens- over-sized & ruby-red coins engraved with the numbers 19 & 21. He slips them into his back pocket alongside his receipts & infront of his wallet. They join another line, this time for the entrance to the permanent exhibition which is titled: "Artists in Residence."

Looking around at their comrades in the queue, Cairey finds a panoply of pairs- old & young, newlyweds & divorces, semblant twins & opposites... some silent, some laughing, some whispering back & forth, & most are looking at their phones, but almost none of them, he notices, are wearing bracelets, & some of these unbraceleted pairs pass through the security check- they are scanned, searched, patted down- but they enter the exhibition unbraceleted. He wonders why this is, & thinks that this might make acceptable fodder for small talk.

"Hey" he asks his date, "how can they get in without bracelets? Do you think they're VIPs? Do they have student passes or something? You know- the last time I was here was..."

She shoots him a quizzical glance.

"No, they're just general admissions. Anyone can go into the main exhibition without a bracelet- well, if they don't want to bring a camera inside. That's just a suggested donation. The expositions are what you have to pay for- & also the photography passes. It's a really smart idea in my opinion, considering you can watch the exhibition from anywhere..."

Cairey fumbles for his receipt & spies the surcharges he hadn't noticed- two photography passes, two tickets to both wings of the exposition... He sullenly says "I don't have a camera or a phone though." She replies "You don't have a phone? Wow. Well, you should have said something. I figured you'd want to take some pictures, I mean-. that's what the MEH is all about- I mean, what would be the point, like, if you didn't have anything to remember? Look-" she raises the selfie-stick- "Smile!"

She smarms & ducks her lips in an overblown ironical fashion. Cairey cringes.

He's avoided being photographed since the night of that afore-mentioned colossal fuck-up- which is etched as deeply in his mind as in the digital panopticon of artificial memory- all the social media posts & ratings from his acquaintance network, his former coworkers, his former peers, all of his "friends"- every bit of data in which he is captured unconsenting, as in every photograph ever taken of him- whenever his face is scanned & tagged & stripped for metadata, exposing how he is seen by others, magnifying his every flaw, & replicating it in-finitely. It is all of these photos that compose the body of his simulated doppelganger- his evil twin, & it is this figure, & not his real self, he thinks, who is truly judged & shuffled about by the almighty forgers of the cybercommercial chains in which he, the innocent one, finds himself so tightly bound & squirm-ing.

In both pictures, as in most pictures, he dons the pained expres-sion of a kidnappee who wishes to convey through the camera lens, to whatever audience receives him, a contradictory com-bination of hope & desperation- a face which begs just as well for ransom as for the merciful deliverance of a bullet through the brain.

She, however, dons that practiced expression from that practiced angle- nearly isometric in its vantage, angled down, from a height above her forehead- a skill that women hone over years of autophotography. She isn't smiling quite- no, it's quite more like a Noh mask- carved precisely to represent, from a high angle, the concept of duplicity- but from a lower & less charitable angle, fraud.

The photograph is taken. The contrast of their mugs is unappealing.

The line shuffles a step forward as a pair gain entrance to the exhibition. With their entrance, the exhibition is deemed to be at capacity, which halts the flow of the line to a dribble.

She frowns at the photo, biting into an unpictured pimple below her lower lip. She's not perfectly pleased with it & it will not accompany her Kale Breakfast Salad & Matcha-infused Green Russian in her social media records. Cairey catches a glimpse of it & is surprised at its resemblance to the last photo of himself he'd seen. He thought perhaps he'd changed since then, that he'd improved since then, but knows better now. He looks even worse, like a boil emerging from an otherwise exemplary specimen of the average human female. Though his companion in the last photo was a different girl, one whose name Cairey could never misplace, which he remembers all too easily despite its complete uselessness in his present circumstance- Helen... She had been his only girlfriend- or at least, sort-of, considering the perpetually "open" status of their commitments. She had been a fixture in his life for several
years, & would have been for several more at the very least, had they not severed on that day of that unfathomably unfortunate fuckup.

His current date bears a slight resemblance to his ex- a diminished doubling, a knock off, or even a parody, kept close like any bargain alternative for the subliminal effect of price anchoring. Even still, her curated stacks of photo-enhancements cannot elevate her to the status of the former. Her nose is larger & less refined in its sculpture. Her eyebrows are too thin. Her eyes are just slightly too far apart. It's as if his ex's face has been stretched & compressed in subtle ways.

These algorithms, he thinks, offer a horrible glance into the sameness of everything- how they pair him with her, again, but with diminishing aura. He looks away from the phone as she meddles through her various feeds. Perhaps, he thinks, they know me better than I know myself. Maybe she's perfect for me. What do I know?

Beside the line is a large plaque commemorating the foundational donors to the Museum of Expressive Humanism. Cairey reads distinguished WASPish names like Jeremen Ingram III, Violette Yates... alongside the names of Saudi sultans, media moguls, tech billionaires, bankers, lawyers, & every sort of person-of-means. He imagines them gathered at some gala, writing checks as if they were signing autographs- the monetary figures entirely unreal to them, except as tax write-offs, accountants' suggestions, or a bored trophy wife's diversions. So many columns of names, like the deceased at a war memorial or the phonebook pages of yesteryear- cacophonies of names stacked in a pyramid formation, accorded position in proportion to investment, & at their peak is- The LaFeint Foundation?

How interesting, Cairey thinks.

He turns to his date, his mouth jutting cautiously agape, his arms raising to get her attention- then - no. She is distracted, flicking through pictures of what he assumes are friends- a girl leaning on the Eiffel Tower, liked- a plate of charcuterie beside a foamy mug of beer, liked- a fluffy cat grumpily glaring from the bottom of a garbage can, liked... the images pass so swiftly he can barely make them out. No- better not, he thinks.

They'd already discussed the show & she was not nearly as devoted as he was & what would be the point? He'd point at the name, she'd say "oh weird" & return to her feed of fragmented moments shared from all across the globe, novelties unending & fluxious, but personally meaningful in their referentiality to real acquaintances- the very opposite of these gilded names of donors, so cold, unchanging, irrelevant & impersonal. No one cares, Cairey.

He glances at the next panel. It is the mission statement of the Museum. Here we go, he thinks, this should be entertaining.

It reads:
 The Museum of Expressive Humanism is unlike any Museum ever before imagined. We have no permanent collections of artifacts. We have no antiquities. We have no gems. What we collect is not "art" as it has been called, but we believe that this old idea of "art" is as anachronistic as monarchy. The King is dead. Art is dead. & what is dead no longer lives. & what is not here for us now, still living, unique & breathing with the vitalistic energy of the human spirit, no longer exists for us.

 What we are interested in collecting, here at the MEH, are living expressions of what is human, by the humans who are living, here & now. We display living Artists while other museums are mausoleums that catalogue the dead. They only look backwards, & we do not. Instead, we look around.

 Try it out. There is no need to consider your visit to the MEH over when you have passed beyond its perimeter. We do not offer sights to be seen. We grant permission to see. Look around you. Revel in the perceptual experience. Every fully embodied moment of humanity's living self-expression is, for us, here at the

MEH, an artistic masterpiece.

Cairey wonders who wrote this shit & what the fuck does it even mean & is it a joke?

The line shuffles forward a bit, as a large group exits the exhibition.

Cairey wonders if he'll get answers to his questions beyond the door. He has a better view now that he's closer to it. He can see the light & shadow spill from its cracks when it's ajar. He can hear the clatter of overlapping voices inside, for a moment, before they are muted by the weight of the door.

She is still flicking through her phone. He passes time by reading the plaque over & over, until it is finally their turn to enter.

She slips her phone back into her purse. They display their bracelets. They're searched. Then the door to the Exhibition is opened for them. Immediately, Cairey recognizes how much it has changed since the last time he'd seen it.

THE EXHIBITION

Originally, in the exhibition room, there had been booths set up like Catholic confessionals. & in these booths, some staffed by "artists in residence" & others by guest volunteers, people could either ask questions provided for them on queue cards or answer them, interacting with whoever their booth happened to contain. The idea, so he was told by his Professor, was that it was an experimental curation of anonymous human interest, of communication-as-such. He had only passed through, as he'd been assigned to review the exhibit & give a presentation on it for his class on "The Politics of Curation."

He'd entered a booth & was asked "How are you?" by an anonymous voice. He'd replied "Fine I guess." He'd thought "Is this really it?" & then asked the anonymous voice the same. It laughed & replied "I think I'm the one who's supposed to ask the questions here. So um, here, it says: 'Are you Art?'" This farce had bothered Cairey so much that he'd stormed out of the booth, the museum, & back to his dorm room, where he wrote a scathing review drenched in irony which praised the Exhibition & the Museum for perfectly exemplifying the vapid totality of human existence & endeavor under Late Industrial Capitalism, which could be summarised as a series of worthless commodities & accidental encounters of bodies in the market, price signals, accompanied by noises in the dark, all amounting to nothing but a colossal waste of time & effort.

His visit to the Museum had been one of the contributing factors to his first change in major, from Socio-Hegemonic

Interrogation & Theory to Aesthetic Praxis & Explication. It was his presentation of his review of the Museum which sealed the deal.

He'd found himself alone in his loathing. While everyone else had cheerfully described some serendipitous encounter with a stranger who had such-and-such touching tripe to say. The more "academic" types used the exhibit as an excuse to furnish a monologue with bits of jargon they'd gleaned from their assigned readings- "something something semiotics something something dissimulation something something challenging radical deterritorializing mimetic something about the Other, the Encounter with the Other, the Mirror reflecting the Other, the Gaze of the Other, to be seen or unseen by the Other, to be or not to be, or not to not to be, but to appear to not to be the Other for the Other in the Otherness of an Other..."- each keyword here lilting in the tone of a question, accompanied by a doe-eyed look to the Professor who nodded approvingly of the word, or frowned, & tapped his pen, until other keywords were proffered- "maybe not the Other as such- but the Shadow of the Other?"- the password guessed, the frown transvaluated to a grin & a nod- the presenter's sentence even ending there, dangling, unfinished, as the words "Good, who's next?" summoned the next paroxysm of puerile pathos or pontification.

Cairey was not well liked. But he was used to this. When it was his turn to present, he'd stood before his peers & said "The Exhibition was stupid. It sucked. It was not Art. It was a waste of my time. I did not understand what anyone here was going on about in their presentations or what the purpose of this assignment was or why it was required of me. Maybe I am an idiot. I just thought that the General Arts Youniversity was supposed to teach us how to draw & paint & make, I don't know, Art?"

He had been cut off here by the flustered gazes of Every-Other, chiefest of whom being his Professor, who had tired of Cairey's insolence & ignorance from day one. He was bothered by his parochial biases, his pretentious dismissals of Ideas which were clearly beyond his ken, his dull refusal of Theories which he refused to engage. He asked Cairey to stay after class. He gave him the suggestion of switching courses & departments to one chaired by Doctor McTeuf, who taught "Material Art History" & gave seminars on the development of technique- seminars which he had been using as a laboratory to draft his ever-forthcoming magnum opus, "The History of Technique," from which only his chapter on the development of pigments had been published, almost a decade prior, which had been so well-received that it got him his position at the Youniversity in the first place.

Cairey's Professor had considered this a devilish prank on his part, as Doctor McTeuf was known as the most boring & anachronistic member of the faculty. To his chagrin, Cairey & McTeuf got along quite well, after the latter had recognized the former's surname from his research into the history of blue dyes.

McTeuf was a very old man, but he had a youthful immaturity about him. He cracked jokes & did not take his work very seriously. Grades were treated casually & assignments were nearly voluntary. In his course, Cairey learned all about the networks that undergirded the production of art through history. He learned about the Phoenicians, & how Tyrian purple, harvested from the shells of predatory snails, supported their often forgotten mercantile empire. He learned about Ultramarine, the mystery of the orient, made of lapis lazuli, & carried by merchant networks across the Silk Road to Europe, where it was reserved for depictions of the holiest of holies, while the less pure azurite, whose color faded in the sun, was used by artists of the less sacred, & that is, less wealthy. He learned about Cobalt blue, which had been known to the Chinese for centuries, but had only been invented in Europe in the industrial era. He learned how it poisoned its handlers, draining them of their iron reserves, & crippling them with anemia. He learned about Prussian Blue, which was an accidental byproduct of alchemy & had been used for everything from blueprints to medicine to poison, as it was, at its core, at the very center of its snow-flake atomic structure, iron, surrounded by cyanide, an element named, wouldn't you know, from the Greek word for blue. He learned about International Klein Blue, invented in the 20th century, which had become considered an art in and of itself, as the conception of art had changed to resemble mass production. Popular culture was itself an expression of this mode of production. The pigment had become the canvas. The product had become the production. This was the end of his course, as McTeuf announced that this was the end of art, an understanding of the techniques of production, no different from the history of beer or wine or furniture or clothes. Once it was shorn of its sacramental ideology, what remained was the transit of commodities & innovations in reproductive industry, & later, publicity.

This mystified Cairey, as no other course he'd ever taken had, but still, there was something he did not understand about it. When he asked McTeuf what the point of it all was, of Art, or its History, he confided in Cairey that he had no intention of finishing the book he had set out to write in his middle-age. He said that he had only ever written enough of it to convince the Youniversity's board that he needed more funding & more time. He said that researching such things was purely a fancy of his, a quirk, a fixation which he'd somehow turned into a career. The book was only a way of supporting his lifestyle.

It was McTeuf who had advised Cairey against pursuing a career in the Arts, nevermind Academia. He told him he would be better off working a more lucrative job & fussing around with paint or drawing or whatever, so long as it was in his spare time- that he'd be much better off making money than spending it on courses- that he could try to make it as an artist if he really wanted to, but really, would be much better off dropping his delusional aspiration of becoming a world-famous, what was it again? Right, a manga artist- as there was no point in making such an attempt in the late industrial age of automation. Soon, he said, you'll be able to train a neural net to produce art based on your own consumer preferences- & when that happens, how silly will you feel having spent so much time on something that could be created instantaneously?

He told Cairey that the only value the praxis of art-making had in the burgeoning era of procedural generation was intangible, nonutilitarian, therapeutic perhaps, but ultimately limited to some private value system which markets could only corrupt. He compared the lot of the human artist in this age to the Buddhist monks who created & destroyed their sand mandalas. To prove the absolute uselessness of contemporary art, he had Cairey guess between amateur artpieces posted online, recently acquired pieces at Modern Art Museums, & procedurally generated paintings produced by nets trained on various aesthetic corpuses. When his eye proved incapable of differentiating any of them, McTeuf laughed & patted him on the back. "After all" he had asked "is art what you've really been chasing? Or has it been that emptiness of mind you once felt as a child, drawing in your notebooks, the total absorption in the void of that eternal present, which creates an illusion of distance from the world? Or have you only wanted to be rich & famous? Because, I tell you kiddo, that ship has sailed. Oh that ship has sailed."

Cairey considered this often ever since. It haunted him like so many things he'd learned at the Youniversity. McTeuf had once warned him: "You're doomed anyway if you can't deploy those keywords you moan about. That's what's produced in this factory here, which they call a Youniversity. They are the passwords to grants, internships, residencies... & considering your aversion, I can't imagine you'll be in any position to become some world-famous artist, whatever that means anymore, hell, you'll be lucky to make a living. I'm often amazed that I've lasted here so long, but then, I have an advantage over you. No one wants to fire an old man when they can just wait for him to die."

It was McTeuf who had shattered his dreams at the time. What he'd said had been hard to swallow, but a part of him had known all of this already. He had at the very least suspected it. The issue was that he had only realized his delusional aspiration for what it was after so many years at the Youniversity. He had gotten himself deep into debt only for him to eventually
graduate in a position no better in talent or aim than when he'd arrived. In fact, the few traditional artworks & virtual projects he had made at the Youniversity had only made him more miserable. They made him question his devotion to making art, to art in general, & further, to the continuance of his own life.

This is what passes through Cairey's mind as he notices that the confessional booths which once composed the Exhibition are long gone. In the time since Cairey's Youniversity days, the MEH has been extravagantly renovated under the new management of the LaFeint Foundation. It now houses the premierest of cyber-anthrotoria.

This means that Cairey sees an immense simulacra of the radiantly advertised midtown blocks that surround the MEH. There are corridors of towers composed of gargantuan- what look like shipping containers- stacked on top of eachother, kept together with a concrete framework, with every exterior face covered in massive television displays which stream the interior exploits of each artist residing in each floor of each tower, from each & every imaginable angle. Guests are able, by means of control boards at the base of the towers, to flick between these camera angles at will, or else, to stream them on their phones. Bluetooth earbuds are available for free use, ostensibly sanitized after being deposited, & they can be tuned to any crate in order to eavesdrop on its cargo, making use of the ubiquitous interior microphones which capture the authentic sounds of each "artist in residence."

Cairey gathers the gist of the conceit. He'd read about this sort of thing opening in Seoul a few years ago. He'd even watched many of its livestreams then, before feeling uneasy with his voyeurism. Livestreams made him feel like a ghost, haunting, for instance, the living room of a Korean girl whose language he could not understand, but whose every action was so plain, so routine, & somehow, so strangely captivating. He had been afraid of how long he could spy on these streams. It condemned his ostensible aversion to them, as he thought such things represented everything he'd come to loathe about the present state of "Art"- that is, the complete dissolution of artist-audience-separation, the obsession with unmediated authenticity, the gawking at artists like they were zoo creatures, turning people blessed with creative talents into dandified pets adopted by anonymous eyes, toddled mobs which treated them like playthings, stuffed animals, dolls, beta fish, to be tossed out, forgotten, or destroyed by the childish whims that govern the affections of spoiled brats with their superfluity of novelties, their continual boredom with an unending procession of surfaces, & so much exposed & half-exposed genitalia...

Cairey thinks about such things as he penetrates the Exhibition. They are thoughts he's thought before. They are hypocritical thoughts, which is something he's also thought before. Truly, he is not so different from anyone else. He knows all too well the drama of rapture & the routine romances of novelty- the momentary bliss of interest, the brief honeymoon period when bliss cools slowly to indifference, to the eventual divorce of disdain, until the next novelty is found, & the cycle is repeated anew. Fittingly, these recirculated ideas fill his mind as he gawks at the first container he encounters, which happens to greet him with a view from a toilet-camera, a favorite angle of the MEH's many accompanied minors.

The angle is bereft, for now, of their scatological hopes. In fact, Cairey doesn't recognize that it's a toilet at all. The bright fluorescence rippling in the humming water of the bowl is dappled like the sun's reflection in a placid pool- close to how its seen as one emerges from its depths for air- or how that's remembered, as in a dream, when the sedimentary flotsam of murk & dirt & microorganisms are erased by the purifying censorship of fantasy, which creates unspoiled views of an impossibly lucid clarity, ungraspable in the living streams of direct sensation...

He loses track of how long he's been lost in the toilet bowl. It strikes him as a beautiful scene. It is simple & pure, as water ought to be. It moves him in the way even the kitschiest of landscape paintings moves him, which is to say, it moves him against his critical judgments. It is only when someone changes the angle to its reverse perspective that Cairey realizes what a fool he's been. He had been enchanted by utilitarian shit-receptacle. He'd even considered it "Art."

All the while, his date has been spinning around slowly, taking in the panorama of screens as a single image, not concentrating on any individual screen or cube, but on the container that contains them all, this warehouse of human exhibition, this cyber-anthrotoria which turned the city into a diorama, with its ceiling-screen televising a livefeed of the overcast sky outside, the sky which contains not only the Museum, but the City, the Continent, & the Globe. She snaps out of her rapture simultaneously with Cairey.

"Let's look around" she says.

So they pass down the simulated streets of this illuminated microcosm, spying on the many sleeping artists in residence through their magnificent digital windows. Though it is just past noon, these artists have lost their connection to exterior time. This is by design. Cairey recalls that when the first of these anthrotoria had been opened,its architect had said something in an interview with foreign press, something like this:

"A: The true artist belongs to no time but his, or her, own. His, or her, time is both his, or her, canvas & his, or her, instrument. In this way, he, or she, is both artist & art. I believe that we have operated under an inverted conception of art for too long, as we imagine the artworks to be superior to the personalities which have created them. This has always seemed absurd to me. It's as if someone were to love a discarded piece of something more than the whole of which it is a part. It would be like marrying, not your wife, or husband, but a collection of her, or his, clipped toenails. It's a form of monsterish fetishism. But my anthrotoria will correct this mistake. They will document the entirety of an artist's personality & their process of production so that the true nature of Art can be finally grasped & appreciated."
"Q: And what is that?"

"A: The true nature of Art is the Exemplary Human Personality in its everyday environment. It is his, or her, carving of himself, or herself, into eternity with each & every irrevocable decision."

"Q: You mean, his 'life-style?'"

"A: Or her 'life-style.' But yes. Precisely that."

They pass through the exhibition, but are not struck by any screen in particular. They inspect them with a passing interest which applies itself equally to the other guests who walk the simulated sidewalks & gawk at the creatures in their electric cages. These are just a few selections of the dozens of spectacles they see.

-A man with a goatee & sunglasses whispering to his partner, a crane-like woman in a beret, who says of a napping artist in residence "he spreads his legs when he sleeps, just like you do" to which the man replies "but he uses his hands like pillows & that's all you!"

-A cube in which a transfemale on her back, masturbates into her own face, which wears a rubber mask (of whom Cairey believes to be Jacques Derrida, or one of those other inexplicable post-modern Frenchman he'd been assigned to read in Youniversity). She holds a portrait of the same face, upon which the word "PHALLOGOUROBOROS" is written in sharpie. This triggers a single stocky lesbian, or transmale perhaps, wearing a fez. She, or he, watching beside Cairey & his date, turns to them, chortling to say "what a joke. He probably never understood what arborescence was in the first place. This is pretentious."

-A disheveled woman in pajamas scrolls through other contemporaneous livestreams, recumbent in bed, eating kettle corn in handfuls, crumbs going everywhere. Plastic handles of vodka filled with cigarette butts are scattered about her room, along with empty prescription bottles, stacks of underwear, pizza boxes, oozing cartons of melted icecream, health bar wrappers, & dozens of cans of seltzer. Cairey's date giggles at this. She says "reminds me of college el-oh-el."

-An ascetic male-presenting skeleton crosslegged in silence, meditating in the center of his absolutely barren cube, which is rendered on screen in the green tint of nightvision. Cairey asks "is he dead?" & his date shrugs.

-A bodybuilding manlet, squatting massive weights, chain smoking, displaying the vascularity of his arms. He's accosted by a recording of his own voice. It accuses him of being a bitch

& a faggot.

-A frenetically naked & gangly androgene coated in layers of spattered paints over a polyester bodysuit, all of which contributes to the fluidity of her(?) gender. She(?) writhes on the floor, crashes against the walls, & smears arcs of putrid browns flecked with colors as diverse as an oily cerulean to a metallic platinum. A hooded man in sunglasses passes by Cairey & his date as they watch this & ask each other "what the fuck?" He turns around to say "I think it's a bit derivative of Pollack don't'cha think? Abstract Expressionism?" He laughs at his own quip then disappears.

-An obese man in a ratty duct-taped armchair playing the original turquoise gameboy color, which contains that iconic Pokemon Yellow cartridge. He's wearing Osh-Kosh corduroys many sizes too small, torn to shorts just below the knees, along with a t-shirt emblazoned with the promotional photo of the Digimon Movie (the American release) which is also too small, & ends just below his supple man-mammaries. He slurps a fruit-by-the-foot as if it were a strand of linguine & washes it down with a Sprite Remix, before huffing a dramatic exhale & restarting his GBC, readjusting his pose on the chair so that his legs go over the armrests, giving him the appearance of an immense baby held by patched pleather arms. All the while, he chants "Nostalgia! The Nineties! Nostalgia! The Nineties!" The audience for this booth groans & disperses when the picture-in-picture which displays his gameplay cuts to black, after having his speedrun ended by a critical hit from Agatha's Gengar in the Elite Four.

The towers in the exhibition are roughly arranged by the interests of their inhabitants, so Cairey has gathered. Turning the corner after the Pokemon player, they pass from "Miscellaneous Avenue" to "Player's Way," finding an immense crowd gathered before the towers which contain what Cairey calls the "Performative Players." No berets or sweaters are to be seen here. Miscellaneous Ave had been belittered with art students on assignment, taking notes, along with a few middle-aged eccentrics- but Player's Way is a sea of wide-eyed children, teens in streetwear, & the scowling adults who have accompanied them to worship their Gods.

The screens show scenes of fantastical banality. Men, generally, in their twenties or early thirties at the most, sit in computer chairs, hunched over desks, mice, & keyboards, softly lit by the immense widescreen arrays before them. But this typical scene is always juxtaposed with a splitscreen showing visions of the wildest fancy- skulls exploding under iron boots, grenades severing limbs, tanks on fire, plumes of smoke rising from smoldering corpse piles, massive armies of science fiction mega-marines mowing down hordes of insectoid extraterrestrial demons, cutified magical girls wielding blades the widths of automobiles winking & giggling while slicing gargantuan hulks in half, medieval knights swinging flails, sorcerers glowing with colored auras, goblin archers, ghastly ghouls, mutilated trolls, decrepit zombies, giant spiders, spaceship laserbattles, trebuchets launching fragments of proscenium arches at the fortifications of besieged cities, gatling guns, dirks, lassos, revolvers, submachine guns, molotov cocktails, grappling hooks, rocket launchers, the crosshairs of bolt action sniper rifle scopes, beasts of lore, gods of antiquity, superheroes from every competing corporate franchise, simulated reproductions of famous athletes, pop stars, cowboys, indians, cops, robbers, hideous nightmare clowns... The entire pantheon of the collective imagination of mankind is represented in the games the players play. All of it is situated together, stitched together like a Frankenstein monster brought to life by the renderings of electricity without any sort of discernible order or criterion of categorization- & from all of these scenes, numbers & scores emerge & clutter the screen, reminding the viewer that all of it's a game. Nothing in these realms could surprise its audience. If a man with the head of a crocodile & the wings of a bird drove a stop-sign honed to a spearpoint through the bowels of a body solely composed of blinking eyes- none would bat their own if it were accompanied with a diminishing health bar, a combo meter, & a voice announcing the end of round three.

No- the only thing that could surprise in this realm of play was something truly unfantastical, that is, something "real," banal & familiar. It would have to be like running into a former acquaintance at a theme park, which would render this person somehow more fantastical & interesting than the surrounding attractions & mascots- & this would only be because his appearance was unexpected. Or perhaps it would be like a parent passing into the magical circle of pretend, demanding acquiescence to chores, routine, & all boring realities of the quote-unquote real world. Contextually, the most interesting part of the game is its player, Cairey realizes here. It is their presence which grants these scenes weight. The players are like the Olympian Gods, & their avatars are merely their disposable dolls.

"Wow" Cairey's date says, as she turns on her heels to get a selfie in front of the crowd. After it's snapped she adds "I never got this videogame stuff or why, like, you'd want to watch someone else play them. You know?"

"Yeah" replies Cairey, unaffected, "It's weird I guess. People must like it for some reason, I mean, look at them."

"But isn't it, like, weird?" she asks, "I mean, you can just play them yourself right? Why would they come all the way here to watch them when they could watch it at home anyway?"

"Yeah. I don't know. I guess so." he replies.

But what isn't weird, really, if you think about it- he thinks- What isn't weird? For some reason people have an innate desire to expunge themselves in the presence of icons. It is not enough to see it. You have to be there, for whatever reason. What was a Museum, ever, if not the site for this sort of adoration? What was a Church? Or a Sport Stadium? What was the Roman Colosseum? What was a protest, or a concert, or Art if not the occasion for this self-expunging, this distraction,& erasure of boring time? How could any of it be differentiated, really? Aren't they all weird from some perspective, if you think about it? How could one means of wasting time & self-erasure be weirder than another without it just being a manner of prejudicial preference based on the peculiarity of an individual's means of doing so? How could anyone explain an act of adoration to someone who doesn't adore what they adore? Is it possible to find some commonality between someone who admires a musician for his musical prowess & another who admires someone fashionable for his taste in clothing? Could it just be that anything exemplary becomes iconic, by some tautological logic, for its exemplary nature- & that these icons stand for the conglomerate masses toiling in uniconic obscurity? Is this what the architect was getting at? Exemplary... He wonders if he has been perversely affected by its curatorial regime. He's starting to think it is right.

But then, more doubts emerge. Couldn't it be some sort of mimetic infection? Is it like a yawn which travels like a wave through a classroom, despite no one wanting to yawn? Do people watch because others are watching? Or is it like when someone points & our eyes are drawn immediately to what they are pointing at? Do people watch because people are born to watch? Or is it like when a dog chases an invisible ball because of his learned response of this gesture begetting that act, for which the pantomime of a thrown ball is no different from the actual? Do people watch because they've been duped into watching? Or does this really satiate them, even though it's fake? Would that mean that everything at bottom is just a means to satiation, simulated or otherwise? How can it be differentiated as authentic or simulated if our brains make no distinction? Is everything just pornographies of various animal wants?

Questions like this bubble without end in Cairey's mind. They never get him anywhere. Eventually, they pop, & disappear, until the next time they emerge. This fizzing fills his head as they walk through the crowd to its most thickly inhabited location, unconsciously drawn, as well, to the focal point, where the reflective eyes of the crowd & the cameras converge upon the most popular figure, charging it with their attention, & thus granting it a supraterrestrial form, some sort of imagined hologram composed of their innumerable vantages, crystallizing their combined attention into the ghostly illusion of a transcendent whole.

"I think that's the one everyone's looking at" his date says, as she points to a screen. He looks at it, even as his brain bubbles with invasive inquiries. They pop.

The figure she's pointed to is sliding into a skintight haptic suit, like a superhero entering his spandex costume, in that halfway zone when his face is not yet covered by the mask, when both of his identities exist at the same time, in the only moment of wholeness- before one identity becomes schizophrenically subsumed by the other, turning it into a secret. If Cairey missed this moment, this figure would have meant nothing to him. He & his date would have passed it by as they'd passed by all the others. But as the crowd cheers in anticipation of this figure's private self disappearing beneath his VR headset, the signal of immanent action- Cairey recognizes the face of this professional player & "artist in residence."

It is Tor Mälmstrom, better known by his gamertag, Set72, which is printed on jerseys worn by a swarm of ecstatic teens in the crowd. Tor had been Cairey's roommate his freshman year at the Youniversity, & he had not thought about him in many years.

They had not been friends exactly, but they had cohabited peacefully- sharing a few moments of intimacy over that year, such as when they'd drink & smoke together, or tidy up their dorm room on Sunday mornings. Tor had changed quite drastically since then. Back in their freshman year, he'd been just as tall & imposing a figure, but now his greasy mane & glasses had been shorn. He's grown a beard he hadn't had then, & he is in rather excellent physical shape, which his haptic suit enhances to a superhuman degree, as each of its heat-&-texture pads glint in the fluorescence of his cube.

His transformation makes Cairey consider how much he has decayed in the same timespan. His own hairline is receding & thinning, beginning to resemble the blonde horseshoe of his father's balding. His skin has started to sag. His stomach now perches over his waistline, though he looks otherwise malnourished. His posture has sloped forward after so many years of deskwork. But way back then, he had still been under the sway of his boundless optimism with regard to his future prospects as a world-famous manga artist. At that time he had even pitied Tor & looked down on him for specializing, not even in videogame design or production, but in "Performative Play" as his major was called, which was the butt of many jokes by other more "serious" majors.

Cairey remembers the most impactful day of their cohabitation. It is a memory he does not recall fondly. It was a Saturday, he remembers, in the middle of a long weekend when no immediate needs constricted his free-time. Tor had been practicing for an extracurricular speedrunning decathlon. He had always been gaming during that year they'd lived together, even without such an event to justify it, but Cairey remembers this distinctly, as it was the decathlon's ruleset, which required analog consoles & outlawed emulation, that explained why in his memory of that day Tor was surrounded in their living room by so many dusty & anachronistic machines.

The rules of the decathlon were that a single iconic game from every console generation would be speedrun, in reverse order, ending on the Magnavox Odyssey edition of Tennis, which was a competitive novelty & rarity for such events, as this final duel would determine the winner & second place finisher from whatever pair finished the other nine-generations first. Tor had already mastered Pacman for the Atari2000, Super Mario Bros for the NES, Super Mario World for the SNES, & was practicing, that Saturday, various backwards longjumps in Super Mario 64 in order to shave his 16 star run into a much more efficient, but nearly impossible, 1 star run.

Cairey, on the other hand, had designated that Saturday as the perfect time to take the amanita muscaria he had traded a similarly psychonautically inclined sculptor for a few of his rare Chlorprothixenes he'd been proscribed in his adolescence before being switched over to Caraprazine. He ate his shrooms with some peanut butter, as was his custom, picking out the nasty bits still stuck in his teeth, swishing water around & swallowing all of it, so that no intoxicating bit went to waste. His plan was to walk around the city in order to find some inspiration somewhere for his end-of-the-year art-project. He had no idea for it, & generally found his inspiration by these means. Otherwise, he only reproduced themes he had drawn countless times before. What he was after was the excitement of "new ideas," & it was these that he sought out in his psychonautical vision quests.

He had decided to leave the dorm room an hour after imbibing the mushrooms, so in the meantime, he sat on the floor of their dorm, & smoked a marijuana infused cigarette while he waited, hoping that this would spur a bowel movement, as his only anxiety on his previous trips had been having to use a public restroom, which usually entailed an interaction with a "real person" in order to gain access, & this usually gave him so much anxiety, as he was shy & poorly socialized even while sober, that the paranoia of being found out sent him on the infernal spiral of a bad trip.

Sitting there & smoking, he watched Tor's attempts without interest, initially, but as one of these cigarettes turned to two, & a third necessitated three more to be rolled as provisions for his hallucinogenic excursion, & then a fourth was lit without any presentiments of cathartic relief, he realized that the effects of the mushrooms were already coming on, & earlier than he'd anticipated, likely, due to the fact that he'd eaten them on an empty stomach. His hands had swollen to comical size & he stared at them in wonder. With a fifth cigarette hanging from his lips, he became entranced by the way the smoke was pulled, like bands of lace, into curling geometries of knots which folded in on themselves & then dissolved into the air. He thought that maybe he could draw these miraculous forms.

His gargantuan fingers trembled as he lifted the delicate miracle of his cigarette to flick the cylinder of ash it had formed into the discarded beer can he'd been using as an ashtray. It was only after this ceremony that he became fully entranced by Tor's gameplay. He followed the wire leading from his controller into the N64, & from there to the dusty CRT Tor had salvaged for the decathlon, & when he followed the wires back to Tor's hands, he saw the iconic tridentine controller melt into his flesh. The flicker rate of the CRT was visible to him now, like a strobe light, within which he saw the figure of a small man emerge, lunging awkwardly backwards into an infinite staircase, over & over & over, until suddenly, he clipped into the texture of the stairs & was blasted through the flimsy set piece of his virtual reality into an infinite unrenderable abyss.

Tor muttered an expletive at this failure & lurched out of his chair to reset the console. The screen crunched into a roar of static- & the sound of this roar punched Cairey in his soul & lingered in his mind, looping without end. He would not be going anywhere, he realized, but to his room, to endure the rest of his trip somewhere safe & blanketed which could contain his fragile ego during what he felt to be the inevitable onset of a very bad time.

The CRT static was accepted by his fragmented mind as a revelation of Hell, a tempestuous surge of damned souls in perpetual torment, decimated into an endless war of pixels black & white, whirling in calamitous cacophonous misery. He had taken the events depicted onscreen as an omen for himself, given to him by the pernicious force that governed his universe as a way of punishing his transgression, a punishment for his artificially induced state of altered consciousness. The infinite staircase was a parody of his life, an unending climb up an inclining corridor, where progress was illusory, & when he turned around to reflect on it, poor plumber, Orpheus, he realized that he had gotten nowhere at all. This infinite staircase was lined on the right with the image of a princess, the eternal feminine, which represented bliss, & love- but on the left reigned the image of the reptile king, the dragon, the tyrant of the natural order, which laughed at his attempts to depose him. & those strange lunges, the glitch Tor was attempting to exploit, represented a turning-away from the struggle up the endless staircase of life in an embrace of the impossibility of progress- & this represented what Cairey had believed his psychonautical experiments to be- as they could propel his soul past the encoded restrictions of endless recursions in thought & in life, into a new world by methods forbidden by the programmer of his universe. But this could just as easily launch his soul, as he had just realized, into an unrenderable void where the only escape was complete severance, & a hard restart, & this was what it meant to be Damned. & he was sure that he was going to be Damned. He was born Damned.

& these thoughts repeated in his mind as his material surroundings pulsed like the internal organs of a gutted fish, hanging by a hook, drowning in the air, flopping in the throes of death. & everything in his field of view seemed to be passing him by too swiftly as he rose from the floor, his cigarette burning closer to his flesh, & he felt like he was on an escalator- & he felt as afraid of this as he had when he was a child & he had believed that his shoelaces would get caught in its machinery & tear him to bleeding pixelated bits!

It is not a comforting reminiscence to say the least. But he manages to snap out of it, before it blooms into another episode & spawns another monstrous fuckup. You're being crazy Cairey, he thinks to himself. No one cares. I don't care. Nothing is wrong.

His date taps him on his shoulder, & he turns to her, & she is smiling at him. For the first time he is pleased that she is with him, & that he is not alone with his thoughts. He is comforted by the idea that she is looking after him, or guiding him to some extent. At the very least she is distracting him from his interior horror. He is thankful for her company. It's as if she has finally picked up on his wish at the ticketbooth, & that she is giving him such a sign as he'd requested.

"Do you want to keep going or?" she asks, extending the hanging conjunction with a fading vocal fry.

"I think I want to see this" he replies, surprising himself with the firmness of his declaration, "I mean, unless you don't."

"Oh no no" she says, "I don't mind. I've never watched this sort of thing before, but my little nephew just adorrrrrres it. It'll give me some clout with him." She giggles at herself. "I'm the cool aunt you know."

Cairey smiles at this, & they share a moment of eye-contact which contains a hint of genuine warmth. Maybe, Cairey thinks, today will be better than I feared.

This thought is interrupted by the booming voice of an announcer asking the crowd: "ARE YOU READY FOR SOME VIOLENT DELIGHT?"

The assembled crowd announces their readiness with gleeful cheers, as Tor, or rather Set72, straps himself into his controller-exoskeleton, produced, Cairey guesses, by a company called Finalest, as this name is printed all over it. It looks to Cairey like a torture device from an alien planet, but to the rest, it is the most aspirational commodity imaginable.

The screen on Tor's tower splits into three, with the top showing Tor's corporeal body confined in the controller rig inside of his cube, the middle showing his first-person perspective on the virtual environment within the gameworld, & the bottom showing an omniscient perspective of the very same gameworld, including the one-thousand players that are gathered, from a birdseye view, in the loading zone where some stretch, some run around & practice their acrobatic movements. Set72 bounces on his knees, throws some punches, & runs toward a wall & into the sort of backflip so customarily shown in kung-fu choreography, to which the crowd cheers. Then he reaches behind his back & pulls out his weapon- a war-hammer engraved with glowing runes which appears to weigh hundreds of pounds, but in reality, as Cairey sees, peeking up to the top screen, his weapon is a steel rod with buttons & a trigger on it & could not weigh more than a curtain rod.

The countdown to the game begins, & Tor's body is lifted into the air by the exoskeleton preparing to drop his avatar, Set72, onto the immense virtual continent that comes into view on the bottom screen. Its procedurally generated & randomized environments range in aesthetic from snowy mountains lined with psuedo-Tibetan pagodas, to megalopolitan sprawl, to wild west ghost towns, bucolic rolling hills, murky swamplands, retrofuturist 1950s highways, corrupt geigerian hellscapes, lovecraftian ruins of crumbling temples which shift & slither impossibly, to fairy-tale forests, to military bases... It represents in miniature all of the tropes of fantasy, mapped in a hyperlinked jumble in encyclopedic fashion, the very archipelago of the collective imagination- a microcosm of microcosms. & on this virtual battlefield, there will be one survivor, a master of combat in every fantastical realm, & he will be rewarded with a prize pot beyond Cairey's fathoming, as it is an order of magnitude more than he's earned in the course of his life, considering that his net worth is debt.

The game begins & Set72 lands at the top of the highest mountain in the land- finding an immense wrought-iron longbow which his war-hammer transforms into with the click of a button. He takes aim at another player, who is gliding toward his turf, & dispatches him with an arrow that sails into his heart. A name in an alphabet Cairey guesses to be Thai is marked dead in the corner of the bottom screen, as the unseen announcers shout, along with the cheers of the crowd: "FIRST BLOOD!"

The third camera cuts to the megalopolis where a quarter of the playerbase has dropped. Fifteen are culled in quick succession by a skyscraper collapse caused by a coordinated explosion at its foundation. Carnage is everywhere & Cairey can't quite follow it, though he finds the spectacle riveting & immediately engaging. He only averts his eyes to look between the three screens.

He checks in on Set72 on the second screen, who is now snowboarding down the mock Himalayas, soaring off cliffs, firing arrows in an acrobatic display that could have been a setpiece in a blockbuster film. Elsewhere, on the third screen, players soar on dragons covered in chrome scales, rockets are fired from helicopters, sniper rifle shots split skulls from immense distances, trip wires set off pit traps, robot suits are melted from napalm bombs- death & triumph, victory & defeat are unfolding everywhere as the playing field shrinks in proportion to the virtual world's remaining population. It is simply impossible to keep track of it all as it unfolds live.

Set 72 survives many close calls. He is hit a few times by various armaments, but heals himself by means of the game's regenerative health system. Players cannibalize the corpses of the dispatched in order to recharge their health & "vigor" (a stat that enables acrobatic feats like jumping over buildings & throwing trees).
After twenty minutes of unrelenting combat the field has shrank by 90% of its scope. & ten minutes later, only ten players remain in the final zone- a lake town which contains a lighthouse for some reason, perhaps a bug in the procedural generation. This lighthouse is where Set 72 has made his perch, providing a highground advantage over his remaining competitors.

He'd dropped the bow a while ago in favor of a gold-plated desert eagle, a quote-unquote Legendary Weapon, which provides one shot kills on enemies of any armor level provided that they are shot in the head. The announcers predict his victory from this fact, as it is the strongest weapon in the game. It would be his first first-place finish, the announcers inform, despite his many top ten & top five finishes over the first season of VIOLENT DELIGHT.

Cairey had never heard of the game until today, nor had he known what a giant his former roommate had become in its community since its launch. He had stopped paying attention to such things, & had not known that Virtual-Reality-Gaming technology had advanced to the degree that it had, as such exoskeleton-rigs were still prohibitively expensive & rare. The designers of VIOLENT DELIGHT were an in-house company owned by Finalest, the manufacturers of this body-consuming controller, & only one thousand machines are in existence at the time, scattered all across the globe. Cairey has gathered all of this from the implications of certain statements of the announcers over the course of the game. He has also gathered some bits of Tor's biography from the chatter of the crowd, & the phone-research of his date. Tor had apparently garnered a cult fanbase from his skill at a variety of games. He had been an "artist in residence" for the past two years, & it was only recently that the MEH had invested in this "Virtual Immersion" console at its launch. It had proved to be their most profitable investment in some time, as it drew young viewers to their streams, & to the Museum, more than any other resident in their catalogue. It was for this reason that Tor had been given a luxurious tower all to himself.

Cairey's date read a biographical summary of Set72 provided by a search-engine which claimed that, unbeknownst to Cairey, he had once been an all-state athlete before he had traded in his athletic pursuits for virtual ones, sensing, as he said in an interview, that the future prospects of esports & performative play were far brighter than the ever-diminishing relevance of traditional ball-and-field sports. His intuitions had served him well- providing his lifestory with a coherent throughline, that in premodern times, could have been deemed Providence. It was for this reason that so many came to expunge themselves in his presence. He was proof that their wildest dreams could indeed come true.

Set72 scores a headshot & two others fall into the encroaching abyss. Then two more stragglers die from bleeding out from wounds sustained earlier, unable to find corpses to feed from. This leaves Set72 in the top five already, assuring him a prize that, being only 5% of the winner's lot, is still twice the median monthly salary. Cairey, realizing this, is taken out of his rapt immersion in the game, as monetary figures so often yank him from his enchantments, like a leash around the neck of a rapturous dog chasing after a bird, believing himself for a moment free, only to be humiliated by the limitations of his chain.

How the fuck could it be possible to make so much money competing in a fucking video game? It seems unreal to him. Absurd, though it is normal now, as he knows. It is his disbelief which is strange.

Wouldn't it be better if the stakes were higher? He wonders. There was more dignity when life & health were on the line, not merely simulated, turned like everything in late industrial capitalism into meaningless numbers. Everything gets turned into a score... Why did every prize, every great significance at the end of struggle, all heroism & courage have to disappear into a number behind a dollar sign? They should reward him with something else, he thinks. Why not make him President or something? Why not give him an island or a city? Why is it always money?

This issue had plagued Cairey from the first moment he had realized what money was, & more, what the lack of money was. This tyranny of currency was some sort of black magic in his mind. It could only be explained as a parody- a joke of some sort played by an uncaring demonic entity far beyond his grasp. It yoked & deflated the noblest of things, rendering them dirty, like any coinage passed in the exchange of so-many hands. He felt it around his neck, dragging him, this means of universal translation, this rosetta stone, pulling him to the depths of immiseration, crushing his fields of singing flowers, his dreams that never come true, all the beautiful things desiccated & trampled in the market. Everything he wants is out of his price range. He knows all too well the limits of his holdings.

What unholy alchemy, this decimating atomism, proving in its endless self-confirming loop, that all is composed of number & measurement- of adding, subtracting, multiplying, dividing, exponentiating- all of these subjects which plagued him in his youth- incomprehensible arabesques of arithmetic which turned all to bits passing through the grist mills of algorithm, their endless decimals, their infinities uncomputable by the weak machine of his flesh- these undulating, oscillating figures which snared life & passed it through purses, wires, & through the very air. He envisioned economy as a cloud of whirling nothingness encroaching upon everything- which when inspected, always retreated, dissipated, forever into a flux of darkness, passing through his outstretched hands like water, steam, or mist.

He was told all his life that these things made sense to people far wiser than he- people born with better faculties of mind, for whom the kabbala of coin proved a natural tongue. He was told this was a language of saints & scientists, too esoteric to explain to meager reprobates like he, who believed their lying eyes & their superstitions of eternal forms, their unchanging paltry wive's-tales of parochial stability. He could not see the beauty in the explosive anarchy, the competitive markets, the wars of networks & forces which composed even the minutest of particles in the galaxies of the real. But surely they who had told him these things could not know it in its totality, could they? Had he really been passed over for election? What ill-god had fated him to this life of benighted ignorance & serfdom? Had he really been born damned?

If this was true, than surely he was cursed from the moment of his birth to perform functions for this demon beyond his ability to exorcise, to even know, & therefore love. Surely he was born damned & his station was to bear his damnation, unjustified to himself, but justifiable somewhere else, to betters of whom he was not party. & then, what difference was there really then in his life & in his death? What could keep him from escaping his sentence? Why live? Why suffer? Why go on at all if it never amounts to wealth? & these questions always resolved in the simplest of answers. No one cares about you Cairey. Take it or leave it.

The crowd laughs at a player who'd lost his footing on the roof of a cabin, dying instantly from fall-damage. & then the crowd roars as another player exploits the propulsive force of a rocket exploding at his feet to fly forward, claymore drawn, to decapitate the player who'd fired at him. Three players remain in total, including Set72, & the battleground shrinks to the size of a city block. Set72 swiftly brains the heroic swordsman, extending the crowd's roar, which resolves in a chant of "Duel! Duel! Duel!"

The arsenals of the final two evaporate, leaving them nothing but their fists. Set leaves his perch at the top of his lighthouse with a gymnastic flourish of flips. His final foe, a Swedish player named Jörmun, replies in kind- performing the popular dance of the day, called the Yung Ko6ruh after its eponymous rapper- a dance which involves grabbing one's crotch with one's left hand, placing one's right hand on the back of one's head, forming a right-isosceles triangle with one's elbow, & gyrating like a belly dancer, in waves, thrusting the hips, & throwing one's head back in a pantomime of satisfactory fellatio.

The crowd chanted the hook of the song, titled "SuhSuh," which went:

Ya bih hin me yuh yuh
She bin wanna fuh fuh
I tella nuh uh uh
Buh bih you can suh suh
Ya bih rollin uh uh
Ya bih gimme suh suh
She gimme thuh suh suh
Bih gimme thuh suh suh

The battleground shrinks even further, leaving the two final players on a dock surrounded by water, which cascades like a waterfall into a yawning & encroaching abyss. They feign punches, approach & back off, all-the-while the crowd restarts their chant of "Duel! Duel! Duel!"

Suddenly Set72 drops his aggressive posture, leans back, & feigns a yawn, & then a glance at an invisible watch on his arm, which he taps. This breaks the chant with a ripple of laughter. Then Set72 turns his back to Jörmun, clearly baiting an attack, which soon follows. Jörmun runs at him with a fist cocked & fires a punch as he comes within arms length- but Set72 ducks it, & using his inertia against him, heaves him over his own shoulders, & paralyzes him in a hold with his punching arm pinned to his back. From there, he easily snaps his opponent's neck, invoking the Victory Tune, & the cheers of the crowd. The game is over.

Tör unmasks & detaches himself from the exoskeleton rig, then disrobes his haptic suit. He puts his discarded sweatpants back on & from there, walks to his amply stocked fridge, emblazoned with one of his sponsors, the energy drink brand Skömm. He takes one for himself, cracks it, & chugs it heartily. He retires to his computer desk & immediately logs on to another game, with a more traditional interface, a turn based grand-strategy game called "Homo Monstrosus" in which the player commands a genetic line of hominids from the dawn of anthropomorphic time, warring against other creatures, other tribes, & the vicissitudes of Nature. "Easy clap" he says to his audience "now let's get these monkeys to the fucking moon boys."

A reel of various highlights & blunders from VIOLENT DELIGHT plays on the top & bottom monitors, & the assembled crowd begins to disperse throughout the Exhibition. Few remain to see the monitors change to the next game, & among these few remaining are Cairey & his date.

"That's all?" she asks.

"Seems so" Cairey replies, somewhat mystified by how little this victory has affected his former roommate. Compared to the fans who had cheered him on, he seems almost bored. He didn't seem to notice that he'd won at all- that he had just earned a prizepot that others would kill for- quite literally kill for, with all of the consequential guilt & paranoia that comes with murder for hire- & yet it seemed to mean nothing to him. He already has everything he could want- a home, small, but equipped with all his life's necessities- a fridge, a microwave, a computer, a desk, a bed, a screen, various VR & AR machines- enough to keep his body alive while he plays & plays, moving from one game to the next, from morning to night. For this life of aristocratic leisure he is beloved & rewarded with riches that he did not need anymore. He has everything & even more is given to him.

Cairey envies this stability, this resolute calm & self-assurance, but then- it is only because he'd never known such a state. He never lost himself, or perhaps found himself, in playing video games. They gave him motion sickness as a child, which had alienated him from his peers. But it was more than just games that he failed in. He was always taken out of his submersion in work, relationships, even leisure, by a nagging sense of pur- poselessness & horror, by some discomfort or nausea, by some question or answer which blew through his momentary fields of joy like a tornado of ice, leaving him alone in a barren tundra, silent, depopulate, & cold- without any sense that any other fate could ever befall him, wishing only that the next mael- strom eliminate himself as well.

"Well?" she asks
"shall we?"

& she leaves Cairey hanging there, staring into the simulated sky, before calling back to him "Well?"

& he is thinking of how strange it all is- how everyone can accept this zoo of man, these stacked cubes of domestic atomism- & is this Art? Is this what Life has become? Is this what remains of the species that once toiled & bled in the fields of history? How can this be real?

He thinks about the designers of what surrounds him, a practice instilled by McTeuf- not just the men who mixed the concrete, but the men who drew the schematics of the cubes, the men who designed the technology that enabled the screens to function, the networks they connected to, the microscopic chips & wires, each the product of someone named in some corporate register somewhere, the softwares, the games in which each texture file was itself the end of an individual's entire day, or week perhaps, or even more- & this was the only process that he knew intimately, having toiled for years on texture files, & many for games that never made it to release, or else, were played & then abandoned within a month.

He wonders what happens to all those patches of unfinished worlds... where did they go? Did the worlds in which they were to compose a part exist anymore? Were they lost forever, or did they exist somehow still, somewhere in their fragmentation? Did they ever exist, as a real destination, or were they only ever patches, which left uncompiled, were nothing but the failures of promises left unfulfilled? Does a fragment remain a fragment of a whole if the whole is never completed? Or are these less than fragments...? What would remain of his work if he died? Nothing, he thinks. No one cares or will ever care Cairey.

"Cairey. Come on, the exposition's starting soon" she says, again, acting the anchor to his ship adrift.

"Sorry, right" he says, & then surprising himself, he asks unbidden "You know something crazy?" Which he immediately answers "I know that guy. That guy who just won. We were roommates in school. A long time ago, we were roommates. I never thought he'd get so huge."

"That's wild" she replies, with a hesitant jerk toward the exit.

"Yeah. We lived together. I know him. Well, I knew him a long time ago. I doubt he remembers me, but maybe he would, probably he would. We didn't talk a lot or anything but- I'm sorry. I was just thinking."

"No, it's alright" she says "that's pretty crazy. You know, the other day I was thinking about this guy I knew once. Well, we were in the same daycare for a while as kids. He's a model now I guess. He was in that ad-campaign? You know? For Flöskel? The one where the guy's afraid to bring the girl back to his place? He has, like, a bare mattress on the floor? You know?"

"Yeah, yeah" Cairey says, nodding again, starting to panic, as this is too coincidental. He feels nauseous. He feels a presentiment of a monstrous fuckup.

"& then he fills it up with a bunch of crap? He gets it all at Flöskel, like, cushions & decorations or whatever. He fixes it all up just in time for the doorbell & she comes in & says something like 'Wow. Usually guys have no taste at all' or something. & she's like 'where did you get this?' as she has something like, I think, a lamp or a painting or something, & he says 'Here & There.' I remember that part because that was the name of the collection they were promoting, at least, I'm pretty sure that's what it was called."

"Yeah, for sure," Cairey replies mechanically, as he actually does know what she's talking about, & knows all-too-well the contents of that campaign.

"Anyway" she says "he was on a billboard for it & I could see it from my window at my old place & it always reminded me of when I knew him at daycare. But I saw him on another one, remember, I was telling you on the ride here. It was the one for SlimsBank which said 'he who signs up with Slims may ask for great rates on loans' & it showed him getting pelted with those huge interest rates." She laughs. "Remember, I thought it was funny because he used to get in trouble when we were kids for throwing rocks at people. We all thought it was hilarious, well, when he wasn't throwing them at us. He was always getting in trouble for it, but isn't that funny? Wild, right?"

"Yeah" says Cairey "That's wild."

THE EXPOSITION

They make their way out of the Exhibition, passing through the security clearance for the first wing of the Exposition. They scan the RFIDs embedded in their entrance bracelets at the door. It opens to a row of elevators. One opens for them, & they enter it. As the door shuts, the elevator explains what they are to behold.

"Good afternoon & welcome to the Museum of Expressive Humanism's current exposition titled Everybody is a Genius: In Life, brought to you by the LaFeint Foundation-" (again Cairey considers what connection there is between Symon & whatever this will turn out to be)- "In order to participate in the exposition, visitors must provide permission for our program to access & curate your digital records. This will allow us to personalize the presentation. Your data will be encrypted & disposed of, so there is no need to worry about its security. The full terms of service contract is available on our website. Pressing the button on the elevator that leads you to the exposition will be interpreted as a confirmation of your consent. If you would not like to enter the exposition, please press the exit button, & a refund will be made available to you at guest services. Would you like me to repeat that?"

"No" Cairey's date says.

"Excellent." the elevator replies.

Cairey does not like the sound of this at all. "Access" & "curate"

& "digital records" are never good news for him. He feels an anxious sweat clustering at his brow, but before he can suggest exit or to press the big red exit button himself, his date mashes the button of consent. A facial scan flicks instantaneously across their mugs with the first jolt of the cabin's descent.

Something worse than the half-intoxicated queasiness of the entryway, & worse than the financial migraines, & much worse than the abstract confusions of the exhibition grips him now. He feels all of the foreboding symptoms of abysmality & future ruin & fuckup- the nauseated panic, the esophageal choke of inexorable embarrassment, the gelatinous knees of humiliation, the swift shriveling of the fearful scrotum, & the flushed heatpangs of total-blush. Just as he's felt some measure of invisible stability in himself, unseen in the anonymous crowd of stream voyeurs, he is being thrust, once more, into a nightmare of nudity. He feels he's doomed to be bound by the spotlight- to become subject to a crowd of eyes glinting like scalpels- their eyes like the eyes of monsters half-glanced in the shadows of dusk.

Oh what a fool he thinks himself now, for lowering his guard like this,for living on in this rapacious torture world, for acquiescing to his torments with each indecision & mistake. He's internally pleading that soon enough his pains will frighten his cowardice away, ennobling him to push the big bloody button of exit. He pictures blue balloons in his tenement room.

"Excellent" the elevator says, as a jaunty tune starts up in the background, a new voice (is that Symon's voice?) introduces the exposition.

"Welcome guests, visitors, friends, to the first part of our latest exposition. We are quite proud of it. We hope that you will enjoy it. Ever since the foundation of the Museum of Expressive Humanism, we have attempted to reorient our visitors' perception on Art. We believe that this exposition might just be our greatest yet in this regard.

"As it says in our mission statement: *'Every fully embodied moment of humanity's living self- expression... is an artistic masterpiece.'* In this latest exposition, we have set out to prove this as conclusively as possible. We hope to prove to you that it's not just the *moment* which is an artistic masterpiece, so is the culmination of every moment which composes a human lifetime. We believe that every single human being's life is equally & uniquely interesting. Every life is no less valuable than any traditional artwork of supposed genius. This is true because every single human being's life is composed of such moments of expression & in the patterns that these moments create we can see the universal distribution of a trait that, in less enlightened times, was reserved for a particular subset of human beings. I am speaking of course of 'genius.'"

"It does not take a supposed 'genius' like Einstein to recognize that this universal human genius is the very source of our complete equality as subjects of human interest, & that is, as works of Art. It is the ennobling i that separates us as individual subjects, though it also includes us in the grand family of our genus. This truth has been hinted at from the very onset of human history in what, in less enlightened times, was called 'the soul.'

"It has only been recently that we, as a species, have achieved a state of technological sophistication so advanced & a state of technological distribution so democratic that we can prove once and for all the existence of this 'soul' without retreating into the darkness of unenlightened superstition, religion, or dogma. It is only now, in our current age, in which every human being leaves a trail of artifacts, pictures, words... all sorts of data & metadata of such rich diversity & insight, that we have been able to translate the lifetimes of human beings, through a universal curatorial algorithm we've developed, into a unique work of art composed entirely of these recorded moments of an individual human's self-expression.

"I know, it's a mouthful. But don't despair. We understand that you might be skeptical, but, we hope to prove this to you. Do not be afraid. Our exposition is a judgment free zone. There is no need to feel scandalized or ashamed or shocked by anything you are about to experience. All of it is equally valuable & insightful. All of it is Art. All of it is Humanity Expressed. Open your Mind. Open your Heart. & say it with me, loud & proud, 'Everybody is a Genius: In Life.'"

"Everybody is a genius in life!" Cairey's date chirps.

"Everybody is a genius... in life" he mutters.

& the elevator doors open.

Immediately Cairey's eyes strike upon what he recognizes to be one of the confessional booths that he'd seen, years ago, when last he'd visited the MEH. Only one remains, & it is placed where one would expect a podium in an auditorium, as the rest of the room is outfitted in long rows of cushioned benches, colored like pews in a new-age church of soft-pastel sentiment. The booth is placed above & before these pews, where an altar would stand, & it is flanked by four wide-screen monitors of equal size- two on each side, stacked one atop the other.

They shuffle to an empty pew & take their seats, joining a scattered crowd, which swells as more & more pour in from elevators on both sides, the new geniuses fitting themselves into the empty spaces among the already gathered geniuses. A faint synth choir plays from speakers somewhere Cairey cannot find. It gives him the feeling of sweating in the waiting room of his therapist, his case-workers, his doctors, & dentists, a sort of calmly carpeted eeriness which parodies his internal alarm. As the last geniuses find their seats, & the flow of new coming geniuses halts, the lights dim, & the voice from the elevator speaks to them all.

"Good afternoon guests, friends, visitors, & most importantly, geniuses! We hope you have enjoyed your visit to the Museum of Expressive Humanism. The exposition will soon be under way. We ask that you remain silent & reserve your applause for the end of each presentation. When it is your turn to present, please make your way promptly to the stage, & take your seat within the exposition booth until you are given the signal to return. If at any time you feel as if you need to leave or go to the restroom, both can be found in an auxiliary hallway to the left. Thank you, & enjoy."

Cairey looks over his shoulder, past the rows of anonymous faces behind him, & spies the glowing exit sign. He wants to run to it. He wants to run through it, run out of the museum, & run as far as he possibly could from it until his weak lungs & legs forced him to quit. But he will not.

His date taps his shoulder.

"I'm so excited" she whispers, shaking both her fists in a display of giddiness. Then she drops the fists. "But I'm also nervous. My friends have simply raved about this exposition, but they said it can be brutal."
"Yeah" whispers Cairey "I- I just don't feel so good is all. It's just-"

"Oh no" she says, pouting with sympathy, "are you ok? Do you need to go?"

"Fine, fine," he lies, against his own will, "I just maybe should have gone to the bathroom before is all- but I think-"

"Oh no" she repeats while she doubles the droop of her pout, "do you need to go?"

This display of empathy works on Cairey, despite his cynicism, & despite his alienation from this date of his whose real name he still cannot recall. For some reason, he still does not want to make her overly uncomfortable, to make himself a burden on her, or to embarrass himself. He pities her for trying with him, for having seen something in him worth wasting time, & hope, & effort, & a Sunday morning on. & as much as he's not attracted to her, & as much as he loathes her, deep-down, for putting him in this position, & as glacial in scope as his submerged antipathy toward her entire sex remains, the warmth of her concern, affected or not, melts his disposition & softens his response.

"I'll be ok" he lies, with the lying smile of feigned courage, "I think I'll make it. I think it was something I ate."

& the exposition starts with the lights cutting out & a searchlight passing over the crowd while a major scale plays repeatedly from the ambient speakers. The music ceases & the spotlight too cuts out.

"Harold Fortier" a voice intones as the spotlight re-emerges on a middle aged man, sitting beside what must be his wife. He looks nonplussed as he sighs & makes his way, illuminated by the spotlight which tracks him through the pews, to center stage & into the exposition booth.

The lights cut out again.

All is dark anticipation.

Then, the top-left screen retrieves a snapshot of a child in a baseball uniform, who grows from youth to adolescence, his jerseys changing colors with the years, his face aging, but its cheesy smile remaining constant. This timelapse repeats on a loop. Then a voice booms:

"SPRING: Green Grass, Brother"

The top-right screen retrieves home video footage, marked with a date from one of the waning years of the previous century, its colors overexposed & washed out, granting the clip a rose-hued halo of nostalgia. It depicts the same adolescent in a Varsity uniform cracking a linedrive to center field, at the bottom of the ninth, at tie game, & the voice booms:

"Summer: Bright Lights, Champion"

The bottom-left screen retrieves & flickers through snapshots of this adolescent, now a young man, beside what must be his wife, both of whom wear baseball jerseys for the City's team (The Prophets) in various locations, holding plastic cups of beer aloft, seventh-inning stretching, kissing framed by the data on the Jumbotron, after what must have been an engagement. & the voice booms:

"FALL: Cheers, Citizen"

& finally, the bottom-right screen retrieves, in higher definition, more home-video footage, but of a slightly different child in Christmas-themed pajamas, a child who must be Harold's son, unwrapping a baseball mitt, cheering, & smiling wide with pride at the camera as he tries it on. & the voice booms:

"WINTER: Victory, Father"

All of the screens play their scenes in unison as the opaque exposition booth becomes transparent, revealing its subject, a sentimentalized Harold, rubbing a tear from the corner of his eye. & the voice booms:

"Harold Fortier, you may rise & depart."

& the geniuses in the pews respond with unanimous applause, as a soft light reilluminates the auditorium, & Harold makes his way back to his seat, where he embraces his wife, whose tears provoke his tears, & more applause from the pews. But it leaves Cairey feeling cloyed, even as he claps dejectedly with the dictates of the crowd. His date is more enthused. She turns to him, as the applause dwindles, to say, simply, "Beautiful."

& such is the conceit of the exposition. It is a sort of multimedia biographical double-haiku procedurally generated for every chosen genius, deploying images & themes mined from their traces on the web. Geniuses rise & depart from the exposition booth. The process is quick, streamlined, & judging by the perpetual choruses of applause, satisfactory enough. There does not seem to be any further curatorial meaning to the order in which the geniuses are selected- it is neither by alphabet, nor by age, nor by theme that they're called. But the next few of them pass like so.

Sarah Brewer, called after Harold, a collegiate gymnast: SPRING: Sunshine, Cartwheel
SUMMER: Schoolyard, Double Flip
FALL: Backyard, Balance
WINTER: Competition, Silver

Jared O'Hare, called after Sarah, a middle-aged consultant with

pitstains on his salmon button- up:
SPRING: Promises, Hope
SUMMER: Failures, Resentment
FALL: Sacrifice, Grief
WINTER: Satisfaction, Rest

Elizabeth Leigh, called after Jared, a divorced former model whose twinkling high-heels clack like the long nails of secretaries tapping on keyboards:
SPRING: Comely, Caring
SUMMER: Sultry, Consuming
FALL: Haughty, Punishing
WINTER: Hoary, Exhausting

It is Elizabeth's exposition which is the first not to be met with unanimous applause. Rather, it's with scattered grimaces, winces, & a silence which echoes only the clack of her high-heels as she scowls her way back to her seat.

"Wow" Cairey's date says "That's pretty fucked."

"Yeah" replies Cairey "Fucked."

Internally he is panicking, now that he knows what could be in store for his exposition. The first crop of geniuses had offended him only in their banality, their bourgeois conventionalism, their conformity to the sort of scrapbooking bathos that makes one groan, but only in the way one groans at a joke with a punchline one has heard too frequently to enjoy.

But this exposition? It was not only unflattering, it was bordering on cruelty, rudeness, & precise personal offensiveness. Worse, it had the unmistakable air of truth to it- otherwise the shock of the crowd was inexplicable. Their red faces, Elizabeth's scowling clack of shame... these were signs of recognition of something more than mere incivility. What sort of judgment was this, which could cut so close to the bone? & oh, what would it make of him? He feels dizzy & ill.

The lights dim & another genius is beckoned to the booth. His name is Lawrence McBrady, & he appears to be a bartender in his late thirties, wearing a branded t-shirt, tight black jeans, & couture sneakers. The exposition implies some falling out with his family over a problem with substance abuse. For him, the voice booms:
SPRING: Privileged, Playful
SUMMER: Rejected, Wrathful
FALL: Scavenged, Woeful
WINTER: Neglected, Fruitless

Then following Lawrence, who sulks to his seat in silence, comes Scarlett Novak, a forty year old nurse whose visage implies a dalliance with cosmetic surgery. For her, the voice booms:
SPRING: Hayfields, Neglect
SUMMER: Hornets, Jealousy
FALL: Concrete, Command
WINTER: Cockroaches, Envy

& so it goes for most of the geniuses, who are called to their judgment, & rarer & rarer are the roaring rounds of applause. The mood of the room becomes solemn, until one man, selected by the spotlight & beckoned by the name of Terrence Johnson, makes a dash to the emergency exit. This is met with boos & jeers.

It surprises Cairey, as he has been comforting himself, as he's been falling to anxious pieces, with the notion that the solemnity of the auditorium represents some form of comradery against the decrees of the exposition & its increasingly moralistic judgments. He has assumed that the other geniuses, who'd never gone so far as to boo or castigate the judged, were keeping their own judgments silent, out of respect, & perhaps out of skepticism toward the veracity of the expositon's curatorial regime. He thinks, or tries to think, that their silence in the wake of these devastating exposes is a form of protest- at least, that's how he's considered his own silence. But he had nearly cheered when Terence fled! He had only done what he most wanted to do & was too cowardly to do.

His date turns to him to say: "What a pussy."

& before he can reply, as the lights dim once again, & the spotlight re-emerges to scan the crowd- the voice booms his name, "Cairey Turnbull," & he is beckoned forth to his public exposition. The spotlight on his head is hot & nearly blinds him. His heart races & his limbs freeze. His mouth dries out & his pores weep. He stands slowly, looking down at his date, who nods her head toward the booth, goading him to his inevitable doom. He looks around at all the synchronized faces & heads, swiveling in unison to face him, pinning him with their collective gaze. He is completely surrounded, on all sides, & he realizes that he is already exposed.

He thinks to flee. He could still flee. Maybe he should flee, but it would change nothing, avoid nothing. It would only confirm their judgment & lose their comradery. The spotlight is already upon him & for this to be undone would require his absence from the exposition itself, from the museum, from his brunch... & it did not end there. If only it ended there.

What was this mere instance of the spotlight's fetters but a particular instance of all the eyes that had ever befallen him? What he wants, he knows, is not a momentary refuge from these enemies, some mere counter-instance of invisibility... What he wants is a complete cessation of the light. He wants total invisibility, complete invisibility, even from his own judgment. He realizes, for the first time, that he does not want to die, as he walks his hangman's mile to his scaffold- what he realizes is that what he wants is to have never been born at all. & he realizes that he has wanted this for a very long time.

He opens the door to the booth with tremulous hands. His stomach churns & he feels the vortex of his digestion turning inside-out. The door closes, & all is darkness inside, riddled with nausea & suspense.

Then a vision appears. A screen divided into quadrants raises from the floor of the booth before him. It is a miniature of the monitors that flank the booth. & as it has been for every exposition of genius, the first to display an iconic moment of his life is the top-left corner, & for him, it shows his most cherished & loathed site. It is a house upon a lake where he had vacationed as a child. The voice booms "SPRING"- & it echoes across the crowd- "Fairytales, Blue."

This is enough to frighten Cairey out of his wits. He sobs, & leaks tears, out of fondness & fear, as ever his memories of his innocence prompted him. This place was the only thing he had ever missed in his life. He cherished it & loved it, but wished its memories away- as without them, the rest of it, the aimless sufferings, the quotidian routines, the wasted times, the labors, the struggles, the consumptions & sicknesses, the fleeting bouts of anxious energy which cleared his ever-encroaching mist of shame & regret, but for moments only, like pleasant dreams interrupted by the morning's alarm, by fantasy-fragmenting necessities, these bores & chores, agendas & groceries, these shattered hopes, these botched sacrifices, this unimpeachable loneliness, this emptiness- none of it would stand in such harsh relief against his few fond memories had they never occurred at all.

It is this illusory precondition of enchantment which pains him more than the disenchantment with which he's grown accustomed- as this lost world denies the reality of his own, or at least it denies its necessity & the necessity of his acceptance of it. These memories condemned him, so he condemns them in return.

Then, the top-right quadrant lights up, displaying selections of his early illustrations, his ballpoint juvenalia, in all their shoddy craftsmanship- their weak outlines, their warped perspectives, their nightmarish hands. These embarrass him in their naivety. He thought he'd eliminated these proofs of his artistic origins, long ago, on that night in youniversity, when he'd hid in the embryo of his bedsheets, frozen in horror at the pretense of his ambition, which could only be salvaged by destroying its vestiges, all of these boxes of his impudent scribbles hidden beneath his bed were like a rash on his soul that he'd cauterize, & cover with the gauze of true accomplishment, emerging from the discarded ashes like a phoenix. He'd sworn that day a new beginning. He'd announced a regime of pragmatism & practice, of realism & sobriety, under which he would embrace the superiority of his disenchanted world, triumph over the illusions of his innocence with an artwork of true magnificence- a monument of scope & fortitude.

"SUMMER: Romance, Blue Blue"

Thus boomed the voice over the salvaged scraps of Cairey's late-acquired seriousness.

Then- horror.

The bottom-left quadrant shows surveillance camera footage of that most monumental of fuckups, that aforementioned day of irredeemable ire, which had caused the final breakdown of his pride & his belief in the power of his resolve to face the daily iniquities of his disenchanted world, his day's commute, his gigs, his trivial apartment, his excursions with his psuedo- girlfriend with all their intimations of psuedo-intimacy, she who he'd worked with, slept with, fought with, sometimes laughed with, but never truly loved. As it was on that day that they had signed a lease on an apartment they would share, when they had commingled the detritus of their lives, their luggages, & boxes, their silverware, their appliances, all together strewn on the vacant floor of the future they would cohabit- that they had set out to buy some odds & ends, decorations, a new lamp perhaps, a curtain rod, champagne glasses, a painting... things that would be owned by them as a singular unit of residence- things that would come to symbolize their now insunderably shared world- it was on that very day that they'd gone to Flöskel, at the time of their "Here & There" collection, which was promoted so ubiquitously across the city- it was there that this security camera had recorded the collapse of their togetherness.

"FALL: Farce, Blue Blue Blue"

Cairey's rapidly fracturing mind cannot contain the entirety of this memory, nor could this footage of his former-self gone mad, slashing the kitsch-for-sale, screaming, threatening innocent bystanders with upraised kitchen utensils, overturn- ing displays, shattering all depictions of tasteful domesticity, crashing through their furnishings, those reified ideals in car- pentry, with their price-tags hanging, jeering, overturned, up- ended, & smashed to bits. No- this was only the surface level of his interior collapse, which defied depiction or exposition in these terms. Though the footage was damning, & the debts, & punishments, & the strikes on his social-credit score he'd incurred for his actions were enormous, they were nothing compared to the damage done to his psyche, within that larger undepicted context, his internal life, with all of its invisible as- sociations, motifs, thoughts, dreams, nightmares, which com- posed the constellations of his personal astrology, which he'd only revealed in part, but never, to anyone, in whole.

Cairey hears some laughter from the pews.

He is drenched in sweat. His head aches & his skin is clammy & cold. He feels vomit preparing itself for expulsion, & he wishes, oh how he wishes he had never been born. He prays to forces he's long ceased believing in. He prays for deliverance. He prays for erasure. He prays for a miraculous correction to the accident of his birth.

& the final scene appears in the lower-right quadrant, & it is strange.

It depicts a map of the Museum of Expressive Humanism with a star on it which reads "You Are (Not) Here"- & the star appears to be located in the room which adjoins the posterior exit of the Museum, & this is somewhere Cairey has never been.

What could it mean? He fears. What awaits him there? Could he face it? Avoid it? Why is his the only expose so cryptic in its symbolism?

The voice booms:

"WINTER: Blue Blue Blue Blue Red"

& then:

"Cairey Turnbull, you may depart."

But Cairey cannot move. There is a disconnect between his desire to move & his abilities. He is shaking from top to bottom, as if he has been locked in a freezer. His face is pale & drained. His eyes are red. His nose is running profusely, & blood drips from his left nostril. As he's revealed to the crowd, there is complete silence.

The pews are full of faces squinting ponderously, chins titled to the side in question, lips scrunched, cheeks puckered- it is like his nightmares of overdue lateness, a sensation at once so familiar & strange, as Cairey knows he his awake, & this had never been the case in his dreams, wherein he always knew that he was dreaming, but dreaming inescapably- the moment of awakening always coming from some jump scare concocted by the hack director of his subconscious, an explosion, a gunshot, a snake-bite- but never from the awareness of his dreaming. His lucidity was always useless, in the daylight as in dreams.

& still he sits there, time warping, space wobbling, & the crowd seems to undulate in waves like the ripples of a curtain in a breeze- he thinks he's having a stroke. His heart is racing & all he can do is sit there, mouth agape in dumb stupefaction, hands clutching the ends of his armrests, hyperventilating as the crowd gives scattered gestures of applause to coax him from his expository throne. It takes a museum employee, hidden in the wings, to come onstage & grab his hand to help him stand, before his self-control reasserts itself in part. He leans on this stranger for support, without ever looking him in the eyes. He's lead back to his seat, to his date, whose face is tinged with horror, concern, & disgust alternating in rapid succession.

She asks: "Are you alright?"
& he replies: "Bathroom."

& he continues to lean against this faceless employee as he's lead out of the auditorium to the sound of scattered, confused applause- the sort that follows any resolved stoppage of play resulting from an injury.

& Cairey is injured alright, most invisibly injured. It is his soul, his mind, his genius perhaps, which is bruised. All of the defenses he's erected against the panging wounds of his past are falling down. All of the strategies he's practiced to ward off his mind's diseases no longer function. Where once stood the rusted iron of his machination, now whirl clouds of dust- his fortifications vaporized by the thermonuclear strike of the truth. In the wasteland of his mind, he knows this to be the case. He feels it- what so long he's been suppressing, by the dictates of his therapists... It is as simple as it is unbearable, & as sublime as it is unholy- this truth.

Cairey senses, & not for the first time, that the entirety of his life is a joke.

It is a joke of irremissible cruelty, but no less compelling for this fact. It is a joke played by something, he knows not what, but something of incomprehensible power. He senses the fundamental unreality of himself, being but a pawn & prop in its play, this comedy of tortures played before a coterie of demonry, both invisible & ultravisible, like any audience in the anonymity of night.

& this- oh lord how it makes sense! How explicable he is to himself in these terms! Yes- how innocent he is in this surmise! How helpless, how frail, how victimized is he in light of this revelation! What hopeless resignation, what relief here, to be slave to this archon of supernatural iniquity. How helplessly, beautifully, reliably doomed!

& Cairey laughs like a madman, salivating even as he sobs, & wipes the phlegm & tears & blood & drool from his utterly maniacal mug. His ribs ache, as his steps become erratic, as he sways in the shoulder hold of his possessor, his deliverer, his fellow prop, & pawn- this stagehand of the furies, who's shuffling him to the bathroom, through its door, into the yellow-tinged fluorescence reflecting off a the bathroom's tiled floor, into the corporate beige of the plasticine cage, to the porcelain mouth where his innards will splay.

He falls to his knees before the bowl & vomits with tremendous force. & in this complete spasm of his innards, he evacuates his immediate awareness, & does not notice the employee's disappearance, his departure offstage, as he's whisked away by the expedient convenience of the infernal author of his woes.

He vomits, then breathes, & spits nasty acrid spits which cling to his lips like strands of a spider web- then he vomits again, & again, with equal force, & less & less of his brunch remains until he's vomiting his emptiness in dry heaves which shake his spine & wrench his ribs & swell his diaphragm to its organic limits- until the expatiation is complete & only the spits remain. His breaths are like the gasps for air of the nearly-drowned. He feels miserable, horrible, & yet- strangely free.

He feels nearly weightless & diaphanous, transparent to himself. He feels a clarity so serene, so pure, that he feels that this must be what it's like to die- that after all the torments of the flesh he'd reach a state of relief so perfectly removed from his agonies that it would render them immaterial like multiplying a non-terminating decimal by zero. It is in this complete nullification of himself that he feels solace. & he realizes this, on his knees, on the cold tile floor of the museum bathroom, before this goblet piled & heaped with the acrimonious slop of his insides- & it is here that he feels himself enlightened.

With his face reflected in the vomit flecked pond of the toilet bowl, he sees the light above enframing him with a halo. & it is here that he decides to constellate his memories. & then he will decide what he will do with them. He'll splay them out & read his entrails for omens. He'll look for patterns suggesting completion in his infernal author's design, & perhaps therein he'll diagnose his intractable position, his fatal nameless illness, which he hopes bears no hope for recovery. & it is thus that Cairey Turnbull, ecstatic & dizzy, slumped in a public restroom, sets out to recompose himself.

First, there is the condition of his birth. It was truly accidental. His parents had not planned to produce a useless eater & killer of joy. They had been perfectly pleased to remain fruitless limbs on their family trees. Both were nearing middle age when Mrs. Turnbull discovered her pregnancy, whose signs she had presumed to be the onset of menopause. By the time her disbelief was overpowered by the accruing evidence, she was too far along, according to her particular school of moral calculus, to fix the problem.

Alas, the parasite had acquired a soul. Mr. Turnbull was none-too-pleased with the news, as he'd been firmer in his disbelief. He'd considered himself quite impotent, as he'd been taking male birth control for years without a single scare. Though, he had worried that perhaps his various slips from his prescribed dosing schedule (a point of contention in the marriage, his forgetfulness) had allowed some sneaky spermatozoa to slip loose, like a kamakazi pilot, to sink the cruiser of his domestic tranquility.

He knew better than to challenge his wife's "compromised position" with regard to the ontological category of this menace, & so he resigned himself to his fate, & eagerly awaited this eighteen year contract's end.

Mrs. Turnbull tried to develop an enthusiasm for motherhood she knew herself to lack, as the very idea of motherhood, with its selflessness, its sacrifices, its silent duties, seemed nothing but senselessnesses in various guises. She was agnostic on the natalist question, while her husband was a dogmatist in favor of the antinatalist answer. Human life had always sickened him. He believed it a mark of virtue to save potential prisoners of the cosmos from the desultory bad-deal of consciousness.

His was an apocalyptic comportment, dashed with a bit of epicurean ethics. He believed the avoidance of suffering to be the only rational philosophy & detested every school of lying huckster who sold particular plans for doing so, though, he remained among their ranks. He believed that most of them vastly underestimated the endemic nature of suffering, & would often, in spirits of dark humor, demonstrate his thesis regarding the implicit courage in the act of suicide- after which he'd glibly call himself an arch-coward, being too afraid to miss some contextually relevant future occasion- the next season of a television serial, the results of an election, a mutual acquaintance's get-together, the death of a hated person- anything at all worked, really, as its purpose was to resolve the tension he'd introduced into the room, & in resolving it, he'd prove himself to be an amusing & sincere person amongst the flocks of humdrum optimists. Yes, it showed his courage, his forthrightness in saying so. It demonstrated his freedom from superstition & taboo. & it was this sincerity & morbid humor which had brought he & Mrs. Turnbull together.

They had met at a hotel bar in Tuscaloosa, after both had been sent to conferences for their vocations. He was an Auto & Boat Insurance Salesman. She managed Public Relations for an Apartment Development Corporation. He'd turned to her at the bar & said "Doesn't this godawful town make you want to kill yourself?" to which she'd laughed & replied "More than usual you mean?" They continued talking, sharing the things they scorned in the world. Soon, they had realized, over margaritas Mr. Turnbull had purchased, that they were from the same neighborhood- & eventually, they found their mutual companies so agreeable that they merged their corporate structures & consolidated their assets. They traveled the world with their vacation hours, & made retirement plans. They would spend their last days pleasantly, on a beach, somewhere within the price range of their savings. They were happy with their partnership- two souls navigating the horrors of the world in semi-suburban luxury. So the news of this unaccounted variable struck a decisive blow to their plans, a blow from which they never fully recovered.

Sometimes Mr. Turnbull became aware of the antipathy this had sown in his attitude toward his son, but he never lacked evidence for the rationality of his disposition. Cairey was anything but a pleasant creature. He destroyed things. He woke them from pleasant dreams. He made them tired & bitter. & worse, he was not normal. His obsessions were alien to his. He did not enjoy sports, fishing, or classic rock. He did not enjoy yelling at the idiots on the news. All he seemed to enjoy were these strange bricklike books of japanese cartoons which he begged for incessantly. He read from right to left. For a while, he thought he was probably gay.

Mrs. Turnbull, on the other hand, developed a sort of stoicism, a wearied resignation which accepted things, all things, with the refrain "What can you do?" She survived the child & endured the destructions he wrought. She played the mediator between the two as Cairey grew into his ornery youth. She deployed all diplomatic means necessary in returning the household to stability & silence. Often, at their most peaceful, Cairey was like a boarder or an employee they'd acquired, who was satisfied by the great american tradition of bi-yearly gift-giving, which functioned in the Turnbull house like a seasonal bonus on top of a more regular wage-regime of chores & allowance.

Contracts governed the house. Mrs. Turnbull wrote them, & the two boys signed them. There was never a question about Cairey's leaving at the end of their eighteen year commitment. They took no interest in suggesting a vocation for him, as both had essentially drifted quite arbitrarily into their respective vocations. They'd both graduated from fairly respectable state schools with degrees in the social sciences. She'd majored in Spanish, & he, in Sports Management.

When Cairey, at age five, under the influence of cartoons, announced that he would be a Knight- they said "Go for it." When Cairey, at age fifteen, under the influence of his comic books, announced that he would become a world famous manga-artist-they said "Go for it." & when Cairey, at age eighteen, under the influence of his guidance counselor, announced that he would be enrolling in the avant-garde & critically respected General Arts Youniversity- they said "Hold on there," & retrieved their financial binder, containing the exact figure of the severance package they'd set aside from percentages retained from his yearly allowance. Beyond this figure, they told him, he would have to procure a loan for himself.

& that is what he did, knowing nothing about interest rates or economy, as he had believed so strongly at the time that he was uniquely gifted & would be immediately recognized as such & compensated accordingly, which he understood to mean extravagantly. His parents were less certain, but they did not interfere. They'd reached their longed-for retirements. They'd already put their suburban home on the market & had their eyes on a remote beachside bungalow in the

South where the temperature was more agreeable. They'd held up their side of the arrangement. Cairey was a free agent now.

Initially, they saw Cairey on those biannual days of festivity, but by the end of his protracted six- year term at the youniversity, even these visits ceased. Their communications dwindled to nearly nothing. The last call he'd had with them had been on his twenty eighth birthday. It had lasted five minutes & was composed mostly of awkward silence.

His parents were neutral props in his biography, & they do not shed too much light on the nature of his private cosmology of solipsistic memory which centers itself on other incidences & characters, most of whom were fictitious. It would be rude to not include them, but they are now out of the way.

Rather, in Cairey's recollections, his thoughts focused more on his rapturous adorations. As a child, his parents had learned that he was easily pacified by entertainments of any caliber. He was provided an unending supply of television shows, documentaries, comic books, cartoons, video games, movies, & website- all available to him on the hand-me-down electronics he inherited whenever his parents upgraded their own. He routinely consumed these entertainments for all of his waking hours. Whenever he was free to do so, he could be found, in his room, glued to a screen of some-sort- or else, reading right to left through those mysteriously prized cartoons.

He fulfilled the basic requirements of his life. He did what was asked of him at school & at home, & generally presented himself as a harmless & forgettable element of both worlds. Infrequently, he would provoke havoc in the household, but mostly, he passed under the radar. His shyness was commented upon, at times, but over the years he'd been able to manage a few fleeting friendships when he found another child who also enjoyed the same entertainments that he enjoyed, & enjoyed, also, re-enacting them in pretend. It was only when these games became play at adulthood that he became alienated again. He only wanted to be a knight, not a marine.

The highlight of Cairey's life in these early years was the familial summer vacation to the lake house they rented upstate, where he was free to roam about the adjacent forest, drink unlimited sodas, & furnish two whole weeks with entertainments, however he pleased, in entirely choreless freedom. (Mr. Turnbull fly-fished, something Cairey found boring & horrible, screaming like a girl whenever a writhing fish was brought before him. Mrs. Turnbull read, mostly, romance novels disguising their bared bodices beneath tastefully minimalist cover-art & titles like "The Unassumed Liability" or "The Client & Patient Relation.")

It was here & it was always here, at the very same lake house each year in the woods on the banks of Lake Lear that their idylls of idleness became icons of timelessness or at least that's how they appeared when they looked forward or back to those times as a respite from their dull lives.

& Cairey especially looked forward to them, as it was there that he met the first Abigail of his life. She was a girl his own age whose parents had made quite similar summer pilgrimages to Lake Lear, to a different lake house, but on the same road- or at least, that's what he'd assumed.

One morning, when Cairey was seven years old, he had been climbing trees, imagining himself to be climbing the ramparts of a besieged city lifted from a manga he was obsessed with titled "Samurai Noname"- when he heard footfalls, snapping twigs, & rustling leaves heading in his direction. As they came nearer he heard a voice mumble-murmuring a gibberish song to the tune of:

La-la, La-la, La-la, La-la--

La-la, La-la, La-la--

& this tune offended the seriousness of his noble mission enough that it broke his enchantment. He yelled down at this intruder "Shut up!" in the sober tone of chivalric boyhood chauvinism.

This startled the girl momentarily, before she spied its source in the canopy above, & recognized that it belonged to a silly boy. So she screamed in response:

LA LA! LA LA! LA LA! LA LA!-

LA LA! LA LA! LA LA!-

& she giggled when Carey replied in turn, shaking his tree by pumping its limbs with his legs, making its leaves crash into each other, screaming back "Shut up! Shut up! Shut up! Shut up! Shut up!"

This battle of wits lasted for a few volleys, before the girl recognized the loop they'd entered, & deployed a new weapon.

"Why should I listen to you" she asked "when you're just a stupid leaf in a stupid tree?"

& this struck Cairey most peculiarly, as he was not a leaf, but a knight errant in a company of honorable rapscallions warring against the evil sorcerer who ruled the realms. He considered correcting her on this case of mistaken identity, but decided that it would be better not to waste his dignity on a stupid girl, so he said: "Well you're a stupid branch on the stupid ground." He was pleased with the cleverness of this retort.

It had stupefied the girl, & she stood there, below him, frumpily biting into her lip with her hands on her hips, squinting up at him in a pose of sophisticated girlhood offense. He believed himself the victor of this exchange until she said: "My name is Princess Branche, & you should bow to me."

This was a real conundrum, as to deny the status of her nobility would entail putting away the persona he'd adopted for good. It was simply unimaginable for a knight errant to disrespect a wandering princess in disguise once her identity had been revealed to him. No longer was this a scenario in which some mere girl was interrupting his quest, this was, quite assuredly, a call to adventure.

So he leapt from his tree & bowed before her, as he knew to be customary for knights in the presence of princesses.

"I'm sorry Princess" he said, "I had mistaken you for a spy of the dark wizard's."

Her scornful demeanor softened at this unexpected display. &

87

so she stretched herself into the character she had invented, & responded.

"I am not a spy. I am Princess Branche & my kingdom has been stolen from me. Maybe you can help me find it. What is your name?"

"I have no name" Cairey replied, lifting a line of dialogue he admired from the manga, "but I will accompany you on your quest."

"I will call you Leaf" she said.

& it was thus that their collaborative campaigns began. They lasted from breakfast to lunch & from lunch to dinner, paused only by the clarion calls of "Cairey" & "Abigail" which dissolved their personas, & severed them as a duo, into two only-children from two separate families, states, & townships. Of these estranged existences, they knew nothing but their secret names, yet these were irrelevant fictions compared to the real scourges that blighted the enchanted realms that surrounded Lake Lear. There was the ogre named Arodnid who dwelt in the cave, the zombies in the brambles, the boogiemen who slept beneath the docks, grabbed the ankles of children, & drowned them. There were the vampires in the fields of skunk cabbage, but worst of all, there was Tinfasel, the dark wizard who had stolen the Princess's kingdom & commanded the evil forces they fought. His only weakness was something Abigail called "The Aphorapt."

What this was, she could not say, but their search for it was the motivating principle of the adventures. Their quests always lead them into conflicts with the various elements of their environment. For three summers they maintained these adventures, fleshing out their world with maps they drew & pictures they sketched, which they shared when they reconvened. & it was this world, this patch of forest & lake with its unending quest for the antidote to Tinfasel, which composed the paradise of Cairey's imagination. It was a paradise that he'd never recovered, as it was in that third summer, on the final day of his vacation, that he'd lost it forever.

They had commandeered a canoe for themselves that the Princess had found abandoned on the public dock. They'd taken it to explore the archipelagos amidst the swampier regions of Lake Lear. & on this canoe someone had carved his name beneath the prow. Luke Mourner, was what it read, but this translated into their fantastical vocabulary as Lucremorn, by means of Abigail's phonetic aphorism. It was she, the Princess, & rightful ruler of the realm, who had the last word on the canonicity of its elements. She named its creatures & its isles. This had not been a problem for Cairey, or rather, for the errant knight Leaf, until midway through that third summer, when he found himself becoming increasingly frustrated by her dictates.

He had drawn a treasure map earlier that spring, in anticipation of the summer, under the influence of another manga, titled "Dragon Crusade." On the map he'd marked an X where the Aphorapt had been hidden, which was, he claimed, on the most distant edge of Lake Lear, where a dragon lived- a dragon that he would slay.

But when he presented this to Abigail, with the surmise that he had found it hidden, far away, on a journey he'd taken alone, she met it with skepticism. She said it was a trap of Tinfasel's, as she explained:

"That dragon is not an evil dragon. He is always misunderstood. I have known him for a very long time. He does not have the Aphorapt, because if he did, I would know about it. What he does have is the secret of the star that fell a long time ago, which brings people back from the dead. It only works once in a lifetime he says. It's no use to us. Besides, he isn't worth bothering. He's always very sad."

& this, though it interested Cairey, bothered him more, as it destroyed the crusade he had, for months, envisioned & practiced for. She compromised with his ambitions by agreeing to explore those distant shores of Lake Lear, which had hitherto been inaccessible to them. It was then that she'd led him to the canoe she had found, which she claimed was a gift from that surly old dragon. With this proof, he acquiesced to her command, but not without a residual bitterness. After all, he began to wonder, couldn't he become a Prince? Or even a King? Couldn't their world, which was seeming more & more to be her world, become his world alone? Thus were sown his doubts of her necessity.

These thoughts festered in his mind at night. He thought of all the freedom he would have if he were to journey on his own. He could start fires, hunt beasts, discover treasures, & be more ruthless than she'd allowed him to be. He could find the Aphorapt alone, or better, he thought, he could ignore its supposed existence entirely. He did not know what use it was to him, this mysterious artifact which he only knew by name. He wondered if it might be worthless. & this thought made him sad, but it felt true, & true in the undeniable way that pain was true. But in the morning, he pretended he had never thought these things, & for the rest of the week he played along with her digressionary episodes, knowing deep down that they'd never come any closer to her fake surmise, as they were truly chasing nothing- nothing at all.

Sometimes he'd sigh or snort at one of her discoveries. Sometimes he'd act like what she saw was invisible to him, as on the last afternoon of that summer, when she spoke to a pixie named Ludenia who lived beneath a rock, he saw nothing but mud & leaves. & when she stood up after listening to its secrets & informed him that Tinfasel had hired a band of satyrs to kidnap them & take them away to a labyrinth at the bottom of the lake, she said this in the affected regal tone of Princess Branche, to the person she'd presumed to be the gallant knight Leaf, but she was met with a shrug & yawn, from a mortally bored boy named Cairey Turnbull, who was scratching symbols into the dirt with the stick that had once been his sword.

"Oh" he replied, "That's crazy."

& when he looked up, she was already gone. They never said goodbye. He heard his name called for dinner, & he left, thinking nothing of it at all.

On his return to the his house for dinner, he decided that he'd finally do it. He decided to follow the treasure map that he'd made for himself, after his parents had gone to sleep. The incompletion of the quest he'd envisioned gnawed at him over the whole vacation, & he had finally thought himself brave enough to go it alone. He felt powerful enough to slay the Dragon & become a Prince.

So later that night, he waited beneath his covers, long after his bedtime, for the cessation of sounds which leaked from the television in his parents' bedroom. He waited a while after that, to be safe, & partially, because he was still afraid.

He thought he had heard a voice in the winds from beyond his window, which seemed to be saying either "No" or "Go"- but which it was, he could not tell. Deciding in favor of the latter, he quietly dressed himself in his daytime clothes, & carried his shoes with him outside, carefully closing the creaky door of the lake house, & entering into a kingdom all his own.

The moonlight beamed in fullness through the dark woods & through the cold while a blustering wind tore through his flimsy cotton shirt as he crept, pausing with each errant sound, each snap & shuffle & animal cry. He persevered to the edge of Lake Lear, to the canoe named Lucremorn, & charted off, alone.

He checked his map in the moonlight, but found it mostly illegible. He knew well enough where he should go- the furthest possible place, on the other end of Lake Lear. They'd only ever paddled along the shore, & never further than a quarter of its circumference in either direction. So it was with trepidation that he pressed on, through the center of the lake, where the water was deepest. It was much harder to row alone. It was very cold out. He regretted not bringing his coat. His teeth chattered, but he pressed on, & eventually he made it to the dragon's lair, tied the canoe to a tree trunk, & ventured into the sparse forest of this remotest isle, terrified & alone.

Here Cairey's memory blurs with the nightmares that recurred for the rest of his life. What he knows for certain is that he'd made it back to the lake house before sunrise, & was found entirely drenched & nearly frozen through- hysterically sobbing, his skin pale & nearly blue. He was on the brink of death. A thunderstorm had rolled through that night, while he was on the dragon's isle, & he had, somehow, made it home through the storm. He was wrapped in blankets & taken immediately to the closest emergency room where he was treated for severe hypothermia. In his delirium he had asked about Abigail, about Princess Branche, & Tinfasel, & Lucremorn- but nobody could grasp what these names referred to. They were merely the glossolalia of a half-frozen boy. His doctors hushed him & were kind enough about it, but even after he recovered he continued to ask about them, & to dream of them.

& in his dreams he found himself confronted on that island by a shadowy figure, which he'd presumed to be the somber dragon he'd come to slay. It greeted him, but by his secret name. "Cairey Turnbull" it said "I have been waiting for you."

"Do not be afraid" it said "I have the treasure you have come for." & this did little to calm him, as the cold glow of the moon cast shadows of impenetrable hues, & the nightwind shrieked across the water, & all was blistering cold.

"Take it" the voice whispered, as a gust of wind whirled a devil of leaves toward a stone which reflected the ghostly blue of the moon. & though he was afraid, he approached this stone slowly, & saw a figure form upon it from the shadows of the looming canopies which danced in the wind. & from these shadows, a crown emerged.

"Take it, my liege" the voice whispered, "& all your dreams will come to life, & all your pains will be relieved, & you will warm this frozen night."

& the crown looked so alluring, like a birds nest cast in obsidian. & it was as light as the air in his hands as he grasped it & lifted it. & as he rested it upon his head, lightning cracked through the night & the sound of rain approached across the lake. & the voice boomed: "Tinfasel!"

This dream recurred, in more or less clarity, for years- always ending with the storm & the voice booming: "Tinfasel!" - which is when he'd wake up, sweating & feverish.

He had another dream too. In this one, he met the somber dragon on the isle, who warned him that the Princess had been stolen by the satyrs & trapped in the labyrinth below the lake. He told him that the only way to free her from their prison was to find the star that had fallen, so long ago. The dragon told him he would be under his protection so long as he destroyed his crown. When Cairey asked it how he could find the star, he'd receive a vision of a firey cloud raining blood- which is when he'd wake up, breathless & cold.

& very rarely, he had a different dream, or he seemed to remember dreaming this dream, a scene that may have come before or after these other scenes in his memory, if any of them had been real- they all may have only been dreams for all he knew. The contents of this dream contradicted the other dreams, as each dream contradicted the others in part, though they all existed in the same frame, the fairyland of his childhood make believe.

It was in this dream that Cairey found himself in Lucremorn, beneath the moon, in the very middle of the lake looking down at his reflection in the water which glowed blue in the moon-light, reflecting the labyrinthine sky of stars. He watched himself take off the black crown of Tinfasel & lay it in the water. He watched it sink slowly, as into shifting sands, to the bottom of the lake. He felt an immense weight lift from him- which is when he would wake up, feeling blissful & free. This was the most beautiful of his dreams.

There was no "Abigail" as far as his parents were concerned. They had entertained his reminiscences as one entertains any of the pretensions of youth- but the older Cairey got, the more worrisome these stories became, as he insisted on their literal veracity. Once, when asked about his "imaginary friend" Cairey became indignant & testified, in a rage, to the reality of "Abigail" who had, for all he knew, been taken away by those very satyrs she'd warned him about, & was trapped in the labyrinth at the bottom of the lake. & the conviction in his voice was not the playful tone of a child, but the doctrinaire assertiveness of a young adult clinging obstinately to his childhood.

It became necessary to prove to him that this was not the case, as the subject had obsessed him more with every year they returned to Lake Lear without Abigail appearing in the woods. Cairey was no use in providing confirmable information, as he knew neither her surname nor the address of the cabin in which her family stayed. Even so, Mr. & Mrs. Turnbull did their best to investigate (although Cairey always suspected that they had done their best to pretend to investigate). They tracked down the guest books for many of the surrounding lake houses, &

inquired with every family they could if they had a daughter named Abigail, as she had lost something her son had found, & they hoped to return it to her (a reasonable alibi). No Abigails were found, & the process was itself enough to silence Cairey's references to this vestigial childhood silliness.

His imagination found other means of expressing itself. His rudimentary maps & drawings became the focus of his life, replacing most of his other means of killing time in the routines of junior high. He filled dozens & dozens of notebooks with drawings using the blue ballpoint pens he received in bags from his mother, who pilfered them from her office. He made flip books out of stacks of post-it notes. He drew thousands upon thousands of things, usually copying them from the comic books he read, but he always returned to three figures, obsessively- a princess, a knight, & a reptilian satyr wearing a black crown.

He had decided the course of his life by then. He never considered a vocation other than chivalry until he started drawing. Then he decided to be a drawer, or "an artist" as it was called. He decided to devote himself to this pursuit entirely, which meant, he came to realize, learning how to turn his drawings into money. This development coincided with his puberty, which had unveiled to him an immense new world of desires, & with them, the parallel universe of the carnal imagination. So he found himself, naturally, stumbling into the role of the classroom peddler of amateur eroticas. He became quite infatuated with the fruits of his black market exchanges in the hallways of his school. He would spend the lunch money he'd receive frivolously on treats, & sometimes, on comic books, or notebooks, pens, & other art supplies. Later, when he entered high school, he spent it on drugs. Being an artist seemed like the greatest thing in the world, but sometimes he got caught.

The first time he was revealed, someone ratted on him after inconspicuously admiring one of his anthropomorphically absurd caricatures of the female form in a state of undress in front of the very generously breasted teacher who it ostensibly depicted which she'd recognized by the helpful caption stating this to be the case in a handwriting she recognized, something of an amateur graphoanalyst, the characteristic close-2 shaped lowercase-a's which belonged to none other than Cairey Turnbull, her quietest student, who sat in the back of the class & read those japanese comic books.

& so Cairey's first of many run-ins with the institutionalized systems of rehabilitation & mental health unfolded. He never quite recovered from the scene of his parents flipping through the collected evidence accrued against their son- their son, the pornographer & creep, who they had never imagined lurking behind the locked door of his bedroom, day to day, producing perversions as his peers played sports & did volunteer work at senior citizen homes (they imagined). He was taken to therapy for the first time, & diagnosed with Attention Deficit Disorder, provided a prescription for miniature doses of methamphetamines, & was scheduled for regular appointments. After this, a new contract was made in the Turnbull household, as a means of correcting Cairey's warped socialization. It required his participation in after-school clubs every day of the week, aside from the day he went to therapy. What these clubs were, they did not care, but as Mrs. Turnbull proffered in one of the stoical gnomicisms she'd grown to love: "Idle hands are the devil's playthings."

Thus Carey entered into the carnival of the social world & learned to cope with its juggling routines. He joined whatever clubs he could find that were tangentially related to his artistic ambitions. He was, by the time he left high school, responsible for a weekly cartoon in the student newspaper (which could be found in nearly every trash of the school). He made graphic designs for student council campaigns, as well as marginal embellishments in the yearbook. He was, otherwise, a frequent guest at the meetings of various interest groups, but mostly, he could be found at the meetings of what was called the "Anime Club"- which was much less a refuge for aficionados of japanese animation & cartooning, than it was segregated safe space for a particular caste of untouchables.

His work for all of these groups took much of his will & effort to accomplish, on top of maintaining his mixed averages in his academic subjects, but somehow he found time to fill his notebooks, on the bus for instance, or during lunch. & still he managed to find time to make money on the side, on commission, & still, these commissions were mostly pornographic in nature. Such drawings, catering to the most intimate of desires, were in high demand amongst that tribe horny alienated nerds who attended the "Anime Club." Cairey was considered one of them by most on the outside- one of those who were to be justly sneered down upon by the stalwart & chosen elect, the future politicians, business executives, lawyers, doctors, & technocrats who attended debating clubs, mock trials, model governments- they who had received the mystery rites that accompanied their inductions into honor societies & varsity teams which enabled them to recognize the damned & reprobate when they saw them, sliming about their halls with their affected strangeness, their stained & awkward fashions, speaking their gawky expressive vernaculars...

Cairey kept a foot in their world, as a fellow traveler of sorts, but he was not considered a citizen by its inhabitants. His tastes were strange to them, even, as he preferred comic books to anime- & he preferred swords & sorcery, dragons, & knights, & princesses, all of the old environments of fantasy- to the more science-fictional & contemporary obsessions of his compatriots. They did not have much in common aside from their alienation & mutual appreciation of alien cultures.

Cairey treated all of his commitments & routines the same way- as necessary impingements on his solitude & his personal struggle with the crucible of art in which he failed, time & again, to produce a nonpornographic artwork which could satisfy himself & a crowd. This was his primary concern in life, & it was this that lead him, eventually, to believe that he could learn a method for doing such a thing, from an institution devoted to such things, as so many of his peers assumed the same with regard to their own ambitions & vocations.

& it was thus that Cairey set his heart on two goals- to move to the city, where there were jobs for artists he was told, & to attend an art school, to receive training in art production which would enable him to be employed as an artist. Both of these were satisfied by his choice of the General Arts Youniversity, which had been one of his few options, considering his middling statistical significance when measured by the metrics that served as the criteria for making such decisions. His art portfolio was, admittedly, nothing special compared to so many other portfolios of similarly amateurish anime-inspired drawings with their cat's eyes, their inhuman proportions, their overly-expressive faces, their romantic themes, & their lack of thematic variety...

& thus did Carey face, not for the first or the last time, the collective computations which governed his socio-economic fate. He learned quite a bit more about this in his youniversity courses. It threw him for a loop, as he had always believed, or perhaps, imagined, that the art world was a refuge from such worldly concerns. He came to realize that it was governed, just as well, by the completely arbitrary tyrannies of the rest of the real world which he had always dreamed of escaping.

He learned about the propaganda embedded in every work of art. He learned about the bondage of the commodity form, the technological & economic superstructures which dictated its collective will, deploying artists as its shock troops. He learned about the violent nature of the artistic eye, the histories of bigoted depictions, the biases of representation, & all about every sort of worldly corruption imaginable. However, despite spending six years shifting majors, he never learned anything about producing an artwork of undeniable quality & genius. Rather, he had learned that this idea of "undeniably great art" & "artistic genius" were entirely contingent, relative, & frankly, anachronistic & delusional in the current age. He learned that supposing such things could exist, or ever existed, their superlative qualities were only recognized for their utility or else the quality of their ideas, meaning, their advocation for a particularly noble societal end. In fact, he learned that this alone was what was worth pursuing in art, as in life, & that artists were no different from any other worker or human being in this respect. He realized, ultimately, that he produced things like all other producers of things, & in his time, these things they produced were quite often not things at all, but virtual representations of things.

These lessons sank in as well as all his other lessons did, which is to say, he knew enough of them to sail by on a C average. Where he ran into trouble was in his peer-reviewed workshops- as while others produced objects which induced consideration on other subjects- such as, the political & ethical legacies of events & figures from previous decades & centuries, or the implications inherent in the categorization of a piece of art as a "plagiarization"- Carey's works induced only cringes, laughter, indifference & confusion over "what it says." Sometimes he received outright condemnation over a particular quirk in his depiction which was taken as a direct personal offense spawned from a hatred he had disguised.

For instance, his attempt to lithograph a horrific & grotesque satyr, wearing a black crown, lording over a cannibal feast, was met with individual disgust & a few partizans debating over the potential heroism or villainy of the depiction of its central figure. Some recognized it as a caricature of the conception of evil found in depictions of the subordinated quote-unquote primitive Other, while others recognized it as a triumph of the marginalized against the dictates of the normalized colonialist & bourgeois majority, as the satyr was quote-unquote primitive & quote-unquote unrefined in his vitalistic nudity (the lynchpin in this case being the fact that one of the corpses on the table wore chinos, dress shoes, & a watch). None of them recognized that this was Tinfasel.

The only question he would ask at the end of his criticisms was the one he'd always asked when peddling his goods- would they purchase the piece, & if so, how much would they pay for it. Sometimes a person would say yes to the first question, but none of them would ever set a price. Cairey presumed, naturally, that this meant his work was a failure. All of his works in his youniversity days were failures.

These sessions always baffled Cairey as he left them less sure of the quality of his work, & of his mind than when he'd entered. It seemed customary for even the most brutal of critical accusations to include a preamble regarding the speaker's subjective enjoyment of some element within the artwork, but the elements they chose seemed entirely trivial to Cairey. "Good job with the grass" was one that stuck with him, as he'd nearly scribbled it on to fill negative space a few minutes before class. He found no correlation whatsoever between the efforts he put forth & the receptions he received. He had even conducted experiments to this end- & found that a doodle could receive more praise for its "expressive minimalism" than his most trying attempts to create "True Art." & still, no one ever offered to buy his work from him.

He was convinced that this was a result of his own inadequacy- as he still, even then, believed that if he truly accomplished his goal of creating a work of "True Art," that it would be recognized, ipso facto, for its undeniable greatness, & consequently, it would provide him a substantial sum of money which would enable him to live somewhere nice, a place he always imagined as that house on the lake. For his attempts to succeed, he had been persuaded, he would require an undeniably great theme or idea- something beyond all that he had made before, his various imitations & regurgitations of his private obsessions or the satisfactions of the intimate desires of others. & it was in this spirit that he'd sought out drugs, stimulants, delirients, hallucinogens, & narcotics of every variety available, as these had been attested by his peers, since high school, to be the source of their creative insights & revelations. Under the influence of these substances, Cairey felt that he'd struck the vein of such themes & ideas, & imagined, always, the resolution of the Princess, the Knight, & the Satyr- but he struggled with translating his private revelations into his craft. Even when he considered himself successful, no one else did.

It was in this pursuit of revelation that Cairey'd procured the amanita muscaria, on that occasion of the worst drug-induced trip of his life, which had convinced him, quite viscerally, of the infernal consequences of his quest to produce such a work of "True Art." It had sent him into a destructive fit, spawned by the terror of his looming failure. He tore the library of notebooks he'd curated over all his years of production to shreds, liberating them from the boxes he'd kept them in, under his bed, only to nullify them in their entirety. He covered his bedroom with a confetti composed of his scrapped compositions, as some sort of apology to the fearful god who punished him for his insolence. In the ensuing panic over his self-destruction, as he came down & sobered up from his mystical intoxication, he felt the dawning of the one truly great theme- a scene that united all his earlier abortive attempts at "True Art."

The project he envisioned was monumental in scope. He would use all of these scraps surrounding him as the bedrock of his composition. He set to work amassing them in piles, elated & enthused with the theme he had struck upon- a perfect recreation of a scene from his most beautiful dream. It was only when he started producing the piece that he'd realize its impossibility.

What he'd envisioned was a complete panorama, which would surround the viewer of his work on all sides as they scanned it from the canoe he would place in its center. It would be from this perspective that the illusion of immersion in his dream would be as complete as he could feasibly fashion given his limited means & talents. He made a rough schematic for the panorama, & decided to break the scene into pieces, & work on it one quarter-arc at a time, as the complete three-hundred & sixty degrees required for the complete cycloramic canvas, at forty feet by three-hundred & sixty feet, would be a lifetime's work, he imagined. So he planned its first installment, a forty by ninety foot canvas, but realized that even this was beyond his immediate time-restraints. So he divided this into two forty by forty-five foot canvases, & set out creating the first.

He used the scraps of his juvenalia as a rough paper-mache scaffolding to express the variations & textures of the environment. He spent two weeks laying just this foundation on the first canvas, which was merely the first half of his first of four consecutive projects. With only two weeks remaining before his freshman year's end & his first final student exhibition, he decided he could only, possibly, finish just this one canvas, & only if he was lucky & diligent.

He used every method he'd taught himself over the years as he spent days upon days skipping class to keep working in his studio space, even sleeping on the floor beside his project. His greatest struggle was mixing the perfect diversity of blue pigments, as in his memory of his dream, floating in the midst of a midnight mist, lost on Lake Lear, everything was soaked in various blues- from the thunderous blue of lightning in the scattered clouds, to the luminescent blue of the moon, to the blue-tinged scatterings of moonlight in the plenitude of wind raised ripples across the surface of the water.

In this first panel, from top to bottom, the composition was planned as follows: the full moon, wholly contained, & below it, the approaching thunderclouds, & then the suggestion of the distant shore obscured through the mist, & then the encroaching fog, & then the ring of water surrounding the canoe. He set to work on it in this order, & on the day before his presentation, he'd only made it to the fog- giving him, roughly, two-thirds of a complete canvas- just over twenty five feet by forty five feet, while a crude, unpainted, fifteen feet by forty-five feet emptiness, filled only with paper mache, pencil outlines, & accidental splatters, composed its bottom third.

This failure disheartened him enough to abandon the absurd scope of his impossible idea, & so he decided to fill this emptiness with a thick & uniform coat of dark, nearly indigo, blue. & after doing this, he felt less pleased with the result than he felt relieved that it was over. He'd never considered how much had to go into an artwork of such scale, such as the one he'd imagined possible. He was certain that it if he had completed it, it would have amazed an audience from its sheer audacity & scope- but he was beginning to suspect that this admiration would only be the subconscious communication, to his audience, of the time & effort it had taken to produce it. He believed that they'd only admire it as much as they'd admire his struggle, the way anyone respects any feat of endurance, no matter its end, with the notion that "I couldn't do that." Worse, he was not sure anyone would buy such a large painting, even if they admired his struggle.

Anyway, he was sure that he was incapable of completing it. No- he realized in his days of toiling how senseless the prospect was. What would he have done next if he had really spent the years he'd need to complete it? What would have been done with it? He wondered. At best it would rot in some museum, or worse, in some storage unit addended to a museum. What would his artwork have changed or inspired in the world? Nothing, he thought, it was not innovative or revolutionary, & its theme was a solipsistic conceit, emerging, probably, from his childhood trauma compensating for itself in narcissistic self-display. This is what his therapist had suggested, anyway, when he had told him about his struggles with completing it. He felt some truth in this summation.

When he presented it, he received the same sort of confusing comments he'd received with all of his works. One person even suggested that the bottom third was superior to the top two-thirds. & still, no one suggested that it was worth any money or wallspace, never mind their own.

Perhaps there's nothing wrong, Cairey thought, with not being an artist, or rather, with being a "creative worker" under the helm of a greater artistic visionary. "Beauty rests in utility" as his mother was wont to say. Perhaps, he thought, he should at least make things that people would pay him for if he could not complete a masterpiece of his own. This was what convinced him to change his major, once more, from Aesthetic Praxis & Explication to Fundamentals of Lighting & Texture, with minor studies in Narrative Architecture, Immersive Entertainment, & Simulation.

Here he learned more marketable skills, though he tended to fare poorly in the classes that extended beyond the "Fundamentals of Lighting & Texture" (which was why he'd ended up majoring in it). He figured that this would be the role he would play in the artworld, & he tried to learn to enjoy it. Often, he found that he did enjoy it, & he began to feel optimistic for the first time since the great disillusionment of his freshman year mushroom trip. With this new attitude, he left the youniversity & entered the working world. He freelanced for various corporations & enterprises, as a sort of temporary worker, fixing up, & tidying assets that others had produced. His panoramic dream was forgotten, & he was only reminded of it, years later, on the most inauspicious day of his life.

In his memory, the years that followed his delayed graduation are chronologically inexplicable- as they resemble a treadmill run through scrolling backgrounds- apartments with half-year leases & jobs that lasted months at most, rendered him an ascetic nomad & scrapper, weighed down by a debt with interest payments that were barely within his penny-pinching grasp. He lived in a state of perpetual fiscal anxiety, & he was wearied over the tenuous nature of his circumstances. He assuaged his anxieties with biweekly drug binges, with alcohol, & with simulated sex. These provided momentary escapes, but ultimately left him with another anxiety, exacerbated by a sense of guilt & shame, for the monetary cost of his consumption, which could never assuage itself without, of course, more money.

He imagined scenarios- absurd deals proffered by the demons of his commercial imagination. He imagined lopping off a limb for money, or selling his blood, or his inessential organs. He contemplated winning the lottery, robbing a bank, coming upon windfall fortunes from the deaths of unknown relatives. He envisioned himself getting rich off of criminal enterprises, selling drugs, producing counterfeit documents- but no such offers or opportunities fell into his lap. Rather, he walked dogs, posted fliers for political candidates, collected signatures for various non-profits, & when he was lucky, worked freelance in the dingiest corners of the art world.

He returned to his pornographic commissions, & produced a few couture eroticas for which he'd seldom not receive his promised pay. More often than not, he received his compensation, as he'd become an infrequent contributor to several subscription services for such couture eroticas. Litigation against those who had reneged on their promised funds was beyond his means, & generally, no contracts had ever been signed. In those years he sometimes designed logos for mobile phone games. He sometimes answered hundreds of thousands of questions for consumer research firms. He sometimes washed dishes in sandwich shops, sorted packages & manned cash registers. One dire December, he spent a weekend collecting cans to make up for the rent he owed the primary tenant of his living arrangement, for the walk-in closet which he subletted.

Eventually, after several years of this perpetual grind, he found a fairly stable job for a corporation called Sinflate, a corporate venture known for cranking out second-rate imitations of industry trends with a pornographic gloss, as well as interactive pornographies of a more original design. He had been offered the position from his portfolio of erotica. It had been offered as a temporary gig, but he was asked to stay after he'd shown him-self to be adept at cranking out large volumes of texture files & models in an efficient fashion. At the time, he'd been subletting a basement nearly two-hours away from Sinflate's office by pub-lic transit, & much of the "go-getter" attitude he displayed was merely a result of the fact that his landlord skimped on heating & his workplace did not. Sometimes he slept beneath his desk.

However, when his coworkers complained about management & compensation issues, Cairey nodded along with them, know-ing the ritual of employee comradery expressing itself this way, but all the while, he was relieved to have a modicum of stability in his income, as well as unlimited access to acrid office coffee. His diligence lead to his promotion after six months to a salar-ied position, which amounted to a meager raise, but entailed an increased workload (which, if he'd cared to do the masochistic mathematics, was effectively demoting his per-hour income)-but this salary enabled him to have documentation reliable enough to get his social credit score high enough that he could sign a lease on a microscopic apartment above a mexican but-cher shop, which was still in the ghetto he'd grown accustomed to living in, but at the very least, offered views of its ends.

His new position switched his department from mobile games to live interaction. He no longer made textures & models for the virtual environments of half-assed cash-grab gameworlds, instead, he designed & polished the various procedurally gen-erated digital skins that covered Sinflate's private courtesans who could be rented for a per-minute fee. They interacted with their clients through virtual reality headsets alone or for an increased rate through interactive plasticine replicas of female genitalia, the most popular model being the aforementioned "Tinkerbell." It was prostitution cleansed of the flesh, made en-tirely virtual, & livestreamed with enough personal attention to -in the opinions of their clients- render the old escort ser-vices & livestream camgirls entirely superfluous.

It was in the office that Cairey met the second Abigail of his life, that aforementioned ex-psuedo-girlfriend of his. She was a "motion capture model" for Sinflate's livestream interactive pornographies. Her real name was Helen Leere. Abigail, or rather, "Abbie Normal," was her courtesan name. & though she was always disguised under a procedurally generated digital skin chosen by her clients, often skins Cairey had designed, she was not inordinately unattractive herself, even shorn of her mascara, piercings, hair dye, & all the other collected trinkets of ostentatious individuality which she dolled herself up in. She had taken a shine to Cairey, or at least, she had taken a shine to blabbing to him ceaselessly on their mutual lunch breaks. Eventually, one Friday, she suggested they go out for drinks, & they ended up back at her apartment, surrounded by her various collections of consumerist ephemera, which were, in her case, governed by an ostensibly politically charged curatorial program which meant that there were pretty-pinkified figurines beside vaguely female-empowering slogans, often about "Sex Workers' Rights"; there were posters of androgynous glam-boys, & a bookshelf of leftover university requirements whose books had subtitles like "Queering the Post-Colonial Reapproriation of Margaret Thatcher as a Feminist Icon" or "Critical Autoethnographical Approaches to the Erotic Literatures of Early 21st Century Fandoms"- & of course, her room bore a faint odor of vaporized marijuana (which they inhaled copiously after drunks), incense sticks (which she lit whenever she entered the room), & decaying fruit (as she was a vegan, except for sushi, which she ate every day for lunch). It was there & then that Cairey, at the age of twenty five, lost his virginity, while wearing an augmented reality headset, to this second Abigail, disguised by a Princess skin he had designed for his own satisfaction.

He did not mind this second Abigail. He often thought he liked her a lot. He even admired her ability to express herself by means of her furnishings. He had gotten used to living out of a single bag of luggage, which contained his few changes of clothes, a sleeping bag, a VR headset, a Tinkerbell, & a battered laptop. He had only recently bought a mattress for himself, secondhand, which laid on the warped wood floor of his unadorned apartment with a single sweat stained pillow & no sheets. His only other possessions were a frying pan, a fork, a bowl, a knife, a towel, a thermos, & a cracked blue lamp he'd found on the sidewalk. He considered her to be pretty well put together compared to himself, & eventually their routine of Friday-night fuckings became as regular as his Monday-morning commute. Often, they served as troubleshooting sessions for the skins he was producing for her clients.

She talked enough for the both of them. She loved to share her opinions. He did not have opinions anymore, at least, not any that he thought worthy of sharing. What he had were questions, unending, ever-multiplying storms of indecision & confusion. He had his personal biases, or fetishes, of course, but he could never find their sources, & so he had no way of organizing them under some totalizing philosophy of aesthetics. He had tried before, many times in youniversity, to explain his reasons for liking or not liking certain things, but always ended up as confused as his interlocutors, or else trapped, defending some position he was not sure he held. Even when he was alone he could not come to a conclusive stance or find some kernel at his center from which he could correlate the chaotic flux of his life & the world. There was always another question, a shadow lurking behind any assertion, & behind this, the shadow of this shadow in the form of an assertion regarding the questionability of the question, & he found that this procession of shadows, if not arbitrarily ceased by his mantra of apathy & indecision, would never end. It was easier to agree, he'd found, with consumer demand. There was no arguing with pornography. There, the customer was always right, & he paid for it.

It was easier to agree with her too, as it was easier to agree with everything anyone said. Agreeing never caused problems. & how much worse was it when he let slip a question! A simple "why?" could cause an avalanche of disagreeable sentiment. A "but so?" had nearly lead to a public incident between them one Saturday morning when she had brought up some recent tragedy she'd read about in the news. It was easier to agree, to nod along, & sometimes assert that he had "never thought about that before" even if he had, & he usually had, it was more agreeable to say that he had not. His time in youniversity had made him skeptical of his own judgment, or lack thereof, as he found that his questions, say, "But what's the point of it?"- made him an enemy, while agreeing or feigning wonderment made him an ally. The only thing he had ever asserted was the importance of "True Art," & his desire to create it- but he had found this, over the years, to be the most questionable assertion of all. It seemed obvious, in retrospect, that Pornography was more important than Art.

He had become fully disenchanted with himself & with the processes of art production as a material practice, as he felt his work on texture art & models only supplied the same be-numbing emptiness he'd felt when he had been a dishwasher, a pamphleteer, & a collector of cans. Even his recollection of working on his botched panorama was no different in kind. It was merely one of his first instances of working uncompensated overtime. & when it came to that "great idea" which he took to mean "the effect of the artwork on its viewer"- he had no faith in his ability to control or curate it. The contingencies of his subject matter, his fetishes so to speak, were as inexplicable & arbitrary as anything else in the world. His knight, & princess, & black crowned satyr were only meaningful to him for their con-nection to his childhood world of imagination, which had been cultivated by the happenstance of having consumed particular comic books at a particular time in which such figures were pre-sented to him. They could just as easily have been cowboys or pirates or superheroes or saints or political revolutionaries or scientists... He'd designed all of these skins before for the satis-faction of an anonymous client. That's all there was to it.

This sort of deconstruction was something he kept to himself, or else, unloaded in his weekly appointments with his ther-apist, who always found a way of turning his questions back around on him. This was how he learned, in the first place, that asking questions was a most disagreeable enterprise. He'd been asked questions for almost two decades by various therapists, & he didn't feel any better for it.

Even so, as he entered his late twenties, & approached his

thirtieth birthday, Cairey's relationship & work-life were more harmonious than they'd ever been before. Everything had been fine enough, predictable enough, routine enough, & satisfying enough, until a year ago, when something he'd seen at Flöskel struck him with an answer to all of his questions that he'd never considered before, & it was this answer that threw him into a disorder that he feared he could never recover from.

It was the re-emergence of that uncompleted panorama of his, which he'd left behind at the General Arts Youniversity- as all works made using any materials supplied by the institution were contractually owned by it, & the canvas & paints he'd used had come from their supply closets- nevermind the fact that he'd had no use for it himself. In those interim years it had been purchased as a piece of a lot when the Youniversity had gone bankrupt & was liquidated & stripped by the procurers of its debts. Collections of student-produced artworks were purchased from the liquidation firm by a company that licensed images for use in the production of movie & television sets. Cairey's piece, under the name "G.A.Y. Paintings Lot #6"- had been licensed by a subsidiary of Flöskel's home decor department for reproduction in its "Here & Now" collection, where it was trimmed to show only the five foot by five foot square in which the moon was depicted. It was renamed "Blue Moon." It became the best-seller in the subcategory of "Misc. Wall Hangings"- & was reproduced thousands if not hundreds of thousands of times.

Cairey had known none of this when he'd gone, a bit hungover & ornery from a frustrated troubleshooting session the night before, with Abigail to procure furnishings for an apartment they'd signed a lease on together. He only learned the process by which his piece had come into Flöskel's possession later, after the ensuing incident. What had happened when he saw it, after drifting through the aisles of Flöskel for over an hour, was later diagnosed as a "manic derealization episode." What had happened was that Cairey had become convinced, viscerally & instantaneously, that his life was a joke. He had become aware, upon seeing dozens of "Blue Moons" hanging, of the total unreality & impossibility of the situation in any reasonable world. Somehow, his painting had become a work of "True Art," shorn entirely from his own authorship of it, & worse, from its compensation. In seeing his painting, now successfully appreciated in the market, being admired by droves who did indeed purchase it & hang it on the walls of their homes, he recognized the hand of an evil god bent on torturing him with ironical inversions of his aspirations & his dreams.

In that instant, everything suddenly made perfect sense. All of his questions were answered with the unfolding of this central kernel, & as it unfolded, he felt that he had been invited in on the joke that was his life & his world. He felt a relief so profound that it was intoxicating. He said "none of this is real" to himself, & began laughing like a maniac. He told Abigail, whose eyes widened in horror & concern & disbelief, that she was not real. He told her, in a jumble of breathless laughter, that she was a parody of his imaginary friend from childhood. He told her that he had painted this painting, this particular "Blue Moon," which he held above his head, & that this painting was from a dream he had had, & that this was all a part of the curse he had been under since the night he had set off to slay the dragon & seize the Aphorapt. He cursed & screamed the name Tinfasel in lamentation. He screamed such things at bystanders, & their reactions made him laugh all the harder. He started destroying the paintings, smashing them against the others, slashing them with a knife from a kitchen set they had decided to purchase. He flipped over displays & wreaked general havok through Flöskel until he saw security guards locking onto him with their eyes.

Then he ran, leaving a trail of destruction in his wake, through the labyrinth of Flöskel's departments, through its cafeteria, & out an employee exit, down a fire escape, where a lone dishwasher was smoking a cigarette on an ostensible bathroom break. From there Cairey ran through the city like a fugitive or a secret agent, hiding behind trees in the park, keeping tabs on passing police cars & pedestrians, looking for signs of his Great Enemy, the infernal author of his ails, the dark wizard Tinfasel. He at once wondered if he'd lost his trail, but knew that escaping him was impossible. He'd never felt so alive & alert as that day when he'd turned against the demon of his fate & ran wild through the city like a uncaged gorilla.

He ignored the calls he received on his phone, eventually tossing it down a sewer grate to send the agents of his enemy astray. It was only hours later, when his mania started to fade in the quotidian crowds & routines of the city, that he realized that none of these people gave a damn for him or for Tinfasel. He realized that they were innocent & that he had clearly gone momentarily insane.

It was then that he passed a film crew filming that final scene of that final episode of Symon. It was this site that convinced him that he'd truly cracked & gone mad before, as the reality of this dramatic production appearing just then & there, with its yellow-tape cordons, its cameras, microphones, & assistants-made him question the answer he thought he'd discovered, as he questioned how it could be that he, & not someone more interesting, someone more compelling, more dynamic, & more heroic, could be the protagonist of the dramatic production of the cosmos. It seemed ridiculous to him that any deity of any caliber should pay him any attention at all, nevermind construct a universe around him, & merely to torment him. It was then that Symon gave his speech, which went as follows:

"I ask you, comrades: What are we gathered here together for? I tell you, it is under false pretences. Do you see? This is nothing but a show, a play of lights & mirrors. This is a fraudulent world of my direction. I am its protagonist. But why, I ask you, why have you gathered here to witness this production of mine? Am I boring you now? Has this show gone on too long? You are free to leave whenever you'd like, yet here you remain. Why? Do you know yourselves? I know. You are drawn here because my reality is more engaging than your waking lives could ever dream to be. Am I wrong? Well, I fear to tell you that this show is at its end, but do not fear overmuch. I have merely grown tired of it. There are better things to be done with this talent of mine. I can create realities which surpass your own. Is it not a crime that this talent should be limited to these serial installments? Is this not ridiculous? I think it is. I do. Do you? Well, I tell you, my disciples, soon, someday very soon, you shall never have to part from my world as it will become your world as well. Do you believe me? I tell you, together, we shall upend that dull reality of yours & replace it with one of my design. There will be no need for false realities then. There will be no need for all of these spurious artifices of inferior craftsmanship. I will invade your humdrum world & turn it into a Paradise. There is only one question: Are you with me?"

& it was then that he realized, listening to Symon's speech, that he was, in fact, as entirely free to create True Art as Symon was, or, he thought, free to create a reality superior to his own. He realized then & there that he'd escaped the clutches of Tinfasel, that ill-god of fate, & that his own lifetime lay open before him, open like an ocean scattered with archipelagos of possibility. He realized that he had destroyed, once again, in a fit of intoxication, a reality he had spent so long to create. He realized that he was perhaps too free to do as he pleased. & this was not a relief. It was far worse than the mania to realize the fundamental apathy this dull humdrum reality had to the reality he envisioned in his dreamworld. It was awful to compare the poverty of his soul to the richness of his aspirations- to compare the fragility of his mind to the sensibility of his fantasies- & to compare destruction he'd wrought against the ill-god of his self-loathing, to the work that remained in the construction of paradise.

He felt dizzy as he considered what he could do next- after all that he had done. There was no going back, no amount of penance could rectify his sunderance of the routine reality he had disavowed in that one moment. Abigail would never understand. He could never explain it to her. It was over. & his job- he could not imagine just showing up to it on Monday as if nothing had changed. In the span of a few hours, he had ruined what remained of his life, & with each wave of recollection of what he had just done, he hated himself all the more, & feared himself all the more, & he felt that he could not trust anything that came from his mind any more, though he believed that, someday, in the future, he might be able to build a new reality & make his dreams come true. So he did the only thing he could think of doing- which was to go to his therapist & have himself institutionalized. He let a faceless bureaucracy handle the fallout of his madness.

Persistent Depersonalization-Derealization Disorder was the diagnosis he received- & with that on top of his persistent accumulation of other mental health disorders over his life, he was given a sentence of three months of monitored living in the institution. He took a plea deal with Flöskel, who charitably cut down their estimation of damages by half after they received Cairey's testimony regarding his authorship of "Blue Moon," the painting which had triggered his manic episode. The rest of the money was taken from his meager savings. He was also fined for lease breaking after Abigail got a restraining order against him & moved in with a friend. This was the path of least resistance, & he allowed these contingencies to be taken care of by others. All he did was sign what the lawyers brought him, with the blue pens they would give him, & then he would return to his Cognitive Behavioral Therapy. For the first time since his Youniversity days, he took up filling notebooks in ballpoint pen with sketches of knights, princesses, & black crowned satyrs. He planned to create a masterpiece- a comic book about the lost lake of his dreamworld.

He seemed to be getting better & was eventually released from the institution with disability benefits, & a requisitioned tenement. Provided that he maintain his dosage schedule & make his appointments with his therapists, he would be taken care of for the rest of his life. Sinflate did not offer him his position back, so when he was set free again, in the Autumn, he lived, once more, as meagerly & as tenuously as he had when he'd first graduated. He never looked for a job.

Sometimes, he wanted to. He thought about regaining normality in his life & becoming a productive member of the 21st century socio-economy- & a part of him did want this- but internally, he knew that his only options were the creation of his masterpiece- his dreamworld & paradise- or a responsible suicide which would keep him from leeching any further on the innocent. The former option proved difficult, far more difficult than he had imagined. He faced an onslaught of self-doubts, as he was still unsure whether or not he believed in art, or in his own dreams anymore. He decided to end his life almost every day, after spending hours tracing & retracing random panels of the comic book masterpiece he'd envisioned in part, only to crumple them, shred them, & bemoan the sheer pointlessness of it all. A month into this, he'd even procured a helium tank, as he'd read that this was the most painless method of suicide, but still he let his indecision rule, & procrastinated on a commitment to either option, opting instead to drug himself to sleep.

Instead, he passed his time like he had when he was child-distracting himself with anything he could find. He figured, eventually, that he would decide one way or the other before his savings dried up entirely, as he could not survive, he'd done the math, on his monthly allotments alone, as he still had his tuition fees to pay. Nor, he thought, could he bear the pressures his bank exerted on his social-credit score. He did not want to grow old like this. After his thirtieth birthday, he decided that if he received some revelation of purpose, an idea which could constellate the knight, the princess, & the black crowned satyr, that he would reconsider his inevitable end. Months passed, & this revelation never came.

Instead, he spent more months as frivolously as he always had when free- watching pirated television serials, old movies, browsing the internet aimlessly, learning all about the structures of immiseration he could not change, subsisting on frozen food, rice & beans- generally killing time until his inevitable killing time arrived. The only true respite from his failed attempts to create his masterpiece was the back-catalogue of Symon. It stirred a long lost joie-de-vivre when he watched it, & rewatched it, as he considered it to be "True Art." He began to think that Simon LaFeint was just born to be a much better artist than he could ever hope to be.

He watched & rewatched it hundreds of times. He analyzed it, & read thousands of pages of amateur analyses of it. But when the last season drew to the inconclusive open-end he'd witnessed in person, he considered this a sign that he would have to make the decision he'd put off for so long- & it was then that he'd decided he'd try- why not- a third option, just to see how it would go. He decided he could enter the humdrum reality of the real world again. He would do this, one last time, before committing to his departure. It was then that he registered for the dating app. It was thus that he matched with this fraudulent third Abigail, whose name he had taken, initially, as a presentiment of the revelation he sought. This decision spurred all of the events that lead him, here, to the bathroom stall outside the main exposition of the Museum of Expressive Humanism, where he was sprawled against a toilet paper dispenser, with a waning bout of derealization, reflecting on his life.

Here he is now. Here is his ugly face, marked with every variety of human sputum, looking back at him from the toilet bowl, begging for a final judgment.

He flushes it down the drain.

He feels, once again, the relief of knowing that he is absolutely insane- a potential danger to himself & others. He is proud of himself for reigning in his destruction. He resolves to finally end it all, & remove himself from the world. He believes this is the best thing that he can do. He is glad he has limited his destruction to himself alone this time. But then remembers her. She's somewhere out there, waiting for him.

& what was her real name?

THE REPOSITIONS

Ophelia Drost looks up from her phone to see that the sound that had provoked her was the bathroom door opening- but it is another false alarm. Again, she thinks that maybe he's left, & left with her coatcheck coin at that. Someone else has exited. She's seen this fellow- & knows his biography, at least in miniature from the exposition. It was sad. She had guessed that he'd lost his wife at sea, tragically, from the way his presentation had gone. He looks like he's been crying. He is the second man to have entered & left the bathroom. Neither of them had been Cairey.

This is where he said he'd be, but he could have lied- but he did not seem to be much of a liar. In fact, she thinks their date has been going quite well, & for him to just leave- well, it seems out of the question- & if he were to come out- right- now- she'd regret her suspicions. He did look sick. He looked very sick, anyway. Must have been the brunch. Maybe he was already sick. Maybe he'd been trying to cover it up for her sake. That's it- she thinks, he's been sick the whole time & that explains it all.

It has been twenty minutes since the end of the exposition. She'd gone right to the bathroom, expecting to find him, but he was not there, waiting for her, as she'd expected. So she waited, frustrated by the fact that he had no cell phone. What sort of person, she wonders, doesn't have a cell phone? He's one of those artist types, she thinks, an artist with a flu. She thinks of him wrapped in a blanket, on a sofa, with a box of tissues nearby- & she's bringing him some warm soup, & he says "thank you." She says to him- "Do you remember when we first met? You were so sick but you came anyway, & we went to the Museum..."

She's always getting married in her mind these days. It's new for her. It suddenly came over her, like a sickness, in the last year. She had never even considered it before, at least, not really. Hormones or something, she guesses. Getting old. Her friends are all married now. Having babies. It just started happening, all at once, & she feels so jealous of them. She used to only feel pity.

She'd never even "dated" before, not really. She'd done her fair share of wooing & screwing, but she'd always been more satisfied with her ability to capture than by the quality of her captures. They were always falling in love with her though. It had been terrible. They tried to tie her down. They spewed compliments & devotion until her rebuffs made them turn sour. Then she was no longer their sweet angel, but a demonic little whore. Typical hypocritical boys.

& they always talked too much anyway. & they were always talking about themselves. Especially the handsome ones, the successful ones, they always showed her their resumes as if they were engagement rings. & the sex had gotten worse. They'd ask for a performance review, only to greet her feedback gracelessly. Useless, really. Boring at best, all these boys she'd toyed with so easily for so long. She'd sworn them off a year ago, after her sister had her second kid. Now she wants a husband.

She wants someone nice, someone less needy, less insecure, less neurotic, more- the only word she can think of is "chill"- which means to her: dependable, static, calm, easygoing, content- perhaps, unambitious? She wants someone who will view their relationship as their greatest ambition. She wants someone to hang out with. She wants a relationship like her sister has with her brother in law. Their lives just seem to make sense to her, organized as they are around the routines of domesticity, a son & a daughter, school schedules, holidays.. But maybe without the kids... But then maybe that could come along, after the wedding. She tries it out: Mrs. Ophelia Turnbull.

She shakes her head at herself, having gone through this visionary disappointment thrice in the month already- imagining her life as Ophelia Dorner, Ophelia Pratt, & Ophelia Kraft, only to get ghosted in the sketching phase of a second date, dissolving their suburban house with two kids & a dog, their small but tasteful rural house with a swingset in the yard, & their brownstone which would have had a hanging garden... But this date was different, at least, it has been different so far. This Cairey's such an odd character, a little rough around the edges, but that was manageable. Boys are easily cleaned up. What struck her was that he was so modest, so agreeable, so intent to listen instead of talk. Not once has she been interrupted- & this she has noted as an extreme anomaly. & his exposition, how mysterious! She knew he was an artist of some sort, but he never brought it up. All those drawings, & that quaint little house by the lake... Well, the security footage was... interesting... but it intrigued her. She wants to know the story behind it, & besides, her own exposition was far from spotless. She wishes he'd seen it, but she'd describe it to him later, that is, if he hasn't already left.

She recalls it to herself again. Spring showed her with her family on Easter, hunting for eggs, her in that little pastel bonnet. Summer showed her in high school, beaming in braces in her field hockey uniform. Fall showed her in college, taking pregame photos with the girls- oh she missed them! & Winter showed a photo of her from last year's unofficial office new years eve party. She was pretending to kiss the lips of a ghost at midnight. It was a long running inside joke amongst her closer coworkers regarding a fictitious entity who caused minor inconveniences in the office. He misplaced pens, crashed email servers, & never made a new pot of coffee when the last one had finished. They called this spirit "Hamlet," which they always said in a posh British accent. Over time, he'd become "Ophelia's boyfriend," because one time she'd answered with his name, as a joke, when a coworker had asked if she had any crushes on any of the office's available bachelors.

She's forgotten the words that went along with the photos, aside from the last one, which she sort of remembers: Winter: Fantasy something... But the message seemed clear to her, with the theme of searching in Spring meeting with belonging in the Summer, & the same mirrored in Fall's relationship to Winter... It obviously implied that she would find a husband. Maybe she already has, but he is missing, poor Cairey, in the bathroom. Maybe he is her Hamlet? But then she realizes that she's back in the loop of her marriage thoughts, & she's alway getting disappointed with them, so she flicks out her phone again.

Jeremy posted another picture of his cat, this time he's sleeping soundly on top of his refrigerator. She likes it. Charlie is upset about the results of an election in his home state, at least, according to the meme he'd posted which showed a cartoon of the conservative candidate shutting a door on a kindly looking cartoon of a young immigrant girl whose t-shirt says "The Future." She scrolls past this one. She doesn't do politics. Abbie posted her feet up on their coffee table with the caption "when the roomie is gone"- an inside joke between them which she responds to with several semi-ironical fuming-angry emojiis. Then it is back to posts she's already seen- her cousin's picture of her baby with a french fry up his nose; her college friend's post promoting her boyfriends midafteroon "chillbeat" DJ set at the Sunrise Cafe; & then one of the ponderable posts of a girl she went to elementary school with who had clearly gone more than a bit off the deep end. Her post reads "Capricorn be like fuck your drama until she be like fuck yeah, drama" along with a cry-laughing emojii & the quoted comment "YAS."

So she flicks off her phone again. She checks the bathroom door again. Then she flicks on her phone again. She opens the web browser this time, which goes to her homepage, a site called "The Daily Affirmation." She's already seen today's- a user submitted story about how the Daily Affirmation had "saved her life." She flicks to her news aggregator, a popular one amongst her friends, who are generally, just to the left of the political center, whatever that means. The headline story is the surprising electoral loss that Charlie had commented on with his reposted meme. Below this are stories about protests in Latin America & Estonia, the Civil War in Tachikistan, another accusation of sexual misconduct directed at Yung Ko6ruh, a video from a Scottish zoo in which a lion cub is nestled amongst ewes- this one she clicks, watches, & then returns to the feed- next is an Op-Ed about the next industries that will be disrupted through automation, then celebrity wedding photos, which she almost opens but doesn't, then the lackluster release of a sneaker which had a PR nightmare upon announcement due to its slogan "The Final Soleution" being deemed insensitive & potentially White Supremacist, despite a spokesman's insistence that it was about their newly patented "smart foam" soles (the slogan was changed to "Mending Soles," the article concludes), then a viral video sensation is covered for the trend of teenagers asking their teachers about the "The Sugondese Revolution," then there is an article titled "Hypostasis of Dissimulation: Symon's Endgame" speculating on the next move of Simon LaFeint after the lackluster finale of his television serial. She opens this one.

The reporter, Afton Selinim, had dug into the assets owned by the LaFeint Trust & found a throughline between its patronage of the MEH; its investment in the Virtual/Augment Reality Gaming corporation, Finalest, which had become a household name in the last year due to the extreme popularity of Violent Delight...; & its major investment in Sinflate, some sort of AR pornography service. The reporter believes that the triangulation of these assets hints at what could be the quote-unquote invasion spoken of by Symon at the end of the show. He hypothesizes that his promise of total libidinal liberation could be the seedbed of some sort of Symon alternative reality game. The reporter then warns that the political consequences of this could not be ignored, considering Symon's much-discussed links to "radical ideas" spawned by a peculiar sect of cyberaccelerationists, known or suspected mystic-techno-fascists &- here she swipes back to the aggregator, as she always does when a journalist warns about some great political danger as a means of harvesting clicks & ad-revenue. It's another video game, she thinks, big fucking deal. TV writers are always making that leap these days. It's just where the real money is.

Her eyes glaze over the rest of the articles, so she switches to perusing sales from her favored clothing outlets. She scrolls, scrolls, scrolls through the virtual closet she peruses every day. No new items are on sale. She scrolls through the next, & the next, & the next- getting lost in her window shopping. Then she thinks she hears the bathroom door open- but when she looks up she finds that it hasn't & Cairey is still nowhere to be seen. Fifteen minutes have passed since the last false alarm.

Should she be worried? She decides to ask the next male she can if he could check up on Cairey, but in the mean time, she goes back to scrolling. She gets a text from her roommate asking "How's the date?" to which she replies "Not bad but I might have lost him lol." "What?" she is asked, "Long story she replies, then adds, "I think he has the flu or got food poisoning or something"- "oh no lol" - "right?" - "your luck smh"- "well" she replies, "we'll see." She closes it but opens it again to ask: "How's the writing?"- she's been working on a children's book of her own, after years of editing others for the publisher they work for. She receives the reply "Don't remind me, I'm procrastinating lol." She replies "Well, that's ok. No rush." Then she receives: "It's just" then "like I can't figure out how to tie this one thing up" then "it's starting to not seem like a children's book really" then "maybe young-adult" then "idk, it's not going well lol." She replies "Awh, well, I'm sure it'll turn out great." She receives: "thanks." Then she goes back to scrolling, but she can't find an unexhausted feed to distract her. She's already used up her typical timesinks. She sighs & flicks off her phone. Then she turns it on to check her reflection through its camera lens. She is disappointed with the breakout she thought she'd covered up. She zooms into it in high definition, inspecting her clogged pores & blemishes as she stretches her facial muscles in the warped poses of makeup application. She pulls the foundation & coverup from her purse & reapplies, with some satisfaction. She switches on the enhancement filter & admires herself- winking, making frowns & other goofy faces.

This is who she thinks she is. This is her true face, she thinks, the one she wears inside. It is unjust, she thinks, that she must be tied to this flesh with its decay & aging. Someday she will be very old. The thought horrifies her. Her disgust sends shudders down her spine. She isn't even thirty yet. She calms herself. She's not eighteen, but she's at least not thirty yet. There is plenty of time. Men still find her attractive. She has no shortage of matches on any dating site. She's on a date right now. She's a seven, at least. She isn't hideous. Maybe she'd been an eight before, but seven is still better than six... much better than five! Her sister was prettier. She was maybe a nine, but she married an idiot, & he was getting fat, & she never recovered from the first kid. Now she's a six. Their pictures are nice though. He is nice enough, even though he's boring & dumb. They will have nice pictures to look at when they are old. The pictures would remain. That's nice.

She remembers that she has her own pictures. She decides to scroll through them. She scrolls through her selfies. She scrolls all the way back to her favorite photo of herself. It's the one she uses as an avatar on her dating apps. In the picture she was twenty one & camping with her college friends upstate. She was in good shape then. All the girls that year had decided to do a fitness regimine together. It had something to do with their anxieties over the end of college. It helped them all feel in control. It was nice. They bonded. In the picture she is wearing yoga pants & an oversized novelty t-shirt for a diner her peergroup had crammed & studied in. She had been taken unaware by an on-again-off-again friend with benefits- he's married now, two kids, lawyer- & she's stretching in the early morning sun, her hair elegantly disheveled, candidly captured from her perfect angle, which makes her beauty seem as unaffected & natural as her surroundings.

She looks at this picture quite often, but can't disever it entirely from the memories it contains, which include all of the fights & hearbreaks she associates with the boy who took the photo, who she had once believed she'd marry, maybe, eventually, someday. Caleb Turner, she sighs at the thought of the name, then restrains herself from her normal response, which is to stalk his social media, either masochistically regretting & lamenting what could have been- or sadistically mocking &

scoffing at the fate she has avoided. He was nice but he was boring- but maybe that's what she wanted all along. Dependable. Around. Doting. She misses the comfort. He was clingy but he was loyal at least. It wasn't her fault. She hadn't been ready. He was controlling, very insecure. She winced at a memory of him crying when she denied his request for an exclusive relationship. "We're nineteen" she said. Well, he got what he wanted. He looks forty already.

She flicks her phone on & off & watches the clock roll into the next minute- five have passed since the last time she checked it. This means she has been sitting in this waiting chair, outside of the bathroom, for nearly an hour. He must have left & he doesn't even have a phone. No one has passed by who she can ask to check on him. This is how she's spending her Sunday, she thinks. At least it will provide her some lunchbreak conversation fodder. She rehearses it:

"He was one of those bohemian types. A bit disheveled, a little shy. We got brunch & it might have given him food poisoning. That's why I never order anything with hollandaise. He might've had the flu, I don't know. Anyway, we went to the MEH- walked through the Exhibition, saw some video game thing. Then at the Exposition, midway through, he got really sick & had to be escorted out. I waited for him outside the bathroom for over an hour only to realize he'd disappeared. & guess what? He didn't have a phone! I know! So anyway I ended up having to go through guest relations to prove my coat was mine, because he had the thingy that- you know, the coins they give you? Anyway. I explained it all like, a hundred times until they gave it back to me. Then I went home, ordered takeout, & took a long hot bath. Just another typical weekend in my miserable life!"

It's definitely good for a few chuckles she thinks. A hot bath & take out does sound nice...She starts to stand, resolved to get it over with, when she sees a man coming down the hall. He's wearing a backpack, a hoodie, sunglasses, & one of those chinese medicine masks. Great, she thinks, one of those weirdos. She almost doesn't, but decides the hell with it. She waves him down.

"Excuse me. Sir? Could I ask you a favor?"

-

Simon LaFeint was not expecting to see her in the halls out-side of the first Exposition. It had been an hour since the day's presentation had ended, & he assumed he'd easily avoid recognition & detection on his way to the second Exposition by means of this auxilary hallway. It is a big day. He's planned it for a very long time, perhaps his entire life in some ways. The critical panning of Symon's finale only rendered his plan all the more delicious. He relished the opportunity to further divide the wheat from the chaffe of his following. How else could he choose his apostles? Only the devoted deserved the treasures he'd promised them. Who else could he trust but the most stalwart & unwavering? Considering how much power they would have in the future, well, should all things go as planned... This girl, does she recognize me? He wonders. He hopes not. He hates taking pictures, fielding questions, all these fakely fawning sycophants. He hates these poseurs who approach him on the street, how they take meeting him to be an "opportunity," divinely granted, to pitch their hairbrained schemes, or else, to get impressions on their social media. Pigs pigs pigs, he thinks, the preamble from his famous sermon in the season two finale. She better not mess me up.

"Yes?" he says.

"I'm sorry, this is really weird, but I've been waiting for my date here for, like, an hour & I think he's inside the bathroom, but I don't know for sure. Could you check on him? Or like, check if he's in there?"

"Sure" he says.

She doesn't recognize him.

"Ohmygod thank you so much" she says.

"What's his name?" he asks.

"Cairey. Cairey Turnbull. I think he's sick or something, or at least, I don't know, he's supposedly in there, but I don't know if he is. I'd appreciate it either way."

"Sure" he says, "Cairey Turnbull."

He recognizes the name. Fortuitous, he thinks, but he is accustomed to such fortune. He was born with it. He expects it & is never left wanting. Shock is the prick of the unprepared & surprise is the prod of the unimaginative- season three, episode four- he'd written that- he'd said it, revealing that he was the thief who'd stolen the grimoire from the archives of the oligarch.

& this Cairey Turnbull, well, he's already gleaned all he could of him from his archives. Since shooting wrapped on Symon, he's been watching the Expositions daily on the hunt for intriguing characters. & this Cairey Turnbull, well, he just might make a decent thirteenth disciple. There are so few who enter the exposition whose life-patterns boggle his algorithm. He investigates these, from behind the curtain. Sometimes there's just a lack of documentation, but other times... There's something like a lost spark, a smoldering ember, hidden beneath the piles of dross. Of course he's been waiting for me, he thinks. All is prepared in advance for seizure- as he'd written, season three, episode one. He'd said it to the oligarch when they were introduced to each other. He had been posing as a magician in order to gain entrance to an elite party of psuedo-occultists. That was something that the pesky critics still hadn't figured out- that there really was a grimoire...

He opens the door & enters. A faucet drips. An airvent whirrs. He checks the stalls. They're all empty, but then, the handicap stall... He can see the soles of boots in the gap between the divider & the tile. He knocks on the door. "Cairey Turnbull?" he asks.

-

Cairey had thought he'd got it together, finally, but he was wrong. He stood, prepared to leave the stall, wash his face, clean himself up, explain to his date that he would have to be going, & then go, straight to his tenement, where he'd leave a note on the door, & end himself, finally, by strapping into that blue helium tank & passing into whatever emptiness awaited him- or maybe, fuck it, maybe he'd go on one last bender before leaving. Why not?- but then he started vomiting again. He felt something struggling to exit his esophagus. It was large, larger than anything he'd eaten, larger than anything that could be left in his insides so thoroughly drained. He thought he was expelling his heart. What a way to die, he thought, what a joke.

But what came out of his mouth, clattering off the back of his teeth & splashing into the clear water, framed by the vomit-flecked porcelain of the toilet bowl, was a ruby red coin which floated to its surface. He stared at it, confused, bewildered, & horrified. It was impossible. He'd truly gone mad, he thought. He had to check. So he reached into the bowl, flinching back once he realized that it was real to the touch. It was impossible. He reached in again & retrieved it. He inspected both its sides. They were embossed with the number 10.

He was insane. This confirmed it. He was hallucinating objects now, objects which he could touch & manipulate. He remembered the coins in his back pocket, from the coatcheck. He retrieved them & compared them with the one he'd just spat into the bowl. They were identical in size, color, & shape. 19 - 21 - 10. What does it mean? he wondered. Surely this was proof that he was insane. Surely this was proof that he was in a truly insane & unreal world. Was this a message from God? From the Devil? From Abigail? From Tinfasel? No, no, he'd simply lost his mind.

He heard the bathroom door open, a man walked to the urinal, pissed, whistled, flushed, washed his hands, tugged at the paper towel dispenser, dried his hands, tossed the crumpled brown ball into the trash & left. He hadn't noticed Cairey. How could that be? Was there really nothing out of the ordinary? Did no one else know what was going on?

& what was going on? He looked at the three coins in his hand:

19, 21, 10. 19 & 21, 40. Ok. 40. & 10. 50. Fifty. Five zero. What does it mean? Ok. 21 minus 10, 11, plus 19, 30. Ok. 30. So what? Or maybe, 19 minus 10? 9 & 21. 30 again. Obviously Cairey. Ten away from 40. Ok. What does that mean? Could it be- maybe 21 minus 19- that's 2, times 10, that's 20. 10 away from 30... It's counting down? Time's running out? What the fuck is going on?

The panic set in again. There was no escaping it this time. He'd witnessed the impossible. In his hands was a miracle in the shape of a coin. He had proof now that his world was unreal. At least, he thought he had proof. But how would he know? Was he really just sitting there, in this bathroom stall, thoroughly cracked? Whispering combinations to himself as he stared into his outstretched hands which really held nothing? How would he know? He laughed from anxiety- laughed until he hiccoughed- hiccoughed until another coin shot from his mouth, bounced off the wall & rolled across the tiles of the bathroom floor.He stopped it with his foot & slid it toward himself. Another coin. Another ruby red coin. He lifted it & saw that it was like the others, but embossed with the number 4.

4. 4. 4. 4... 4 & 10 & 19 & 21. 4 times 10, 19 plus 21, 40 & 40. Not this again. Not this again Cairey. 4 coins. The fourth coin is 4. Why? What does it mean? "What does it mean?" he asked aloud. "What am I supposed to do?" The door opened again, & he froze. He felt immediately that he was supposed to hide. He had to hide from whoever this was. He had to hide the coins, so he hid them, back into his back pocket, & perched on the toilet bowl, crouching so his feet were invisible to whatever monster had intruded on him.

This intruder washed his hands. He splashed water on his face. He said: "It doesn't mean anything, ok? It was just a presentation. It was just a stupid fucking gay art bullshit, fuck- It doesn't mean anything. Don't freak out. You're fine. It's going to be fine. You'll turn it around. You know that. You ARE turning it around. You promised yourself. You said you wouldn't think about it anymore. You're fine. Don't do this." He splashed more water on his face, then grunted. "How did it know? No. Don't. Don't do this again. Don't think about it. It was a coincidence. It was just an innocent coincidence. There's no way it could have-" He grunted again. "But how? How did it know about- about-" He moaned. "It doesn't make any fucking sense! How the fuck did it know? How did it know? How did it fucking know?" He turned the faucet all the way on. "Calm down. Ca-alm down. Down. Breathe." He was whispering to himself frantically. He breathed, slowly, long deep breaths, exhaling loud enough to be heard over the faucet's blast. "No one else knows. No one else knows. It was just a presentation. A bunch of strangers. They only saw- they only saw a picture, that's all. It was a picture. & what was it? What was it? It was just a picture. Ok. He also said WINTER: OCEAN BURIAL but that could mean tons of things, tons of things, tons. It could mean- y'know. It could-" He smashed the faucet off. He grunted, then screamed. "IT HAS TO END! IT HAS TO END! I CAN'T TAKE IT ANYMORE!" Then he slammed his way out the door, & disappeared.

The silence that followed was interrupted by sporadic drops from the faucet, marking each second that passed. Drip... Drip... Drip... Cairey was still perched on the toilet bowl, like a gargoyle, clutching the sides of his head. The exposition was driving people insane, he thought. He wasn't alone. It wasn't just him. Maybe- maybe that's all, he thought. Maybe- but the coins. The fucking coins. Forget about the coins, he thought. Don't even look at them. Don't even think about them. Let's just get cleaned up & get out of here. He left the stall & looked at himself in the mirror.

His dirty blonde hair stuck to his forehead in leaves of sweat while the rest of it burst out electrically- like he'd rubbed a rubber balloon on it. His hazel eyes were bloodshot. His pupils were dilated. The rings of his nostrils were caked with dried blood, vomit, & mucous. His skin was pale & flushed at the nose. Right, he thought, I forgot. He hadn't shaved well & the asymmetrical patches of a pubic beard by his ears & under his chin stood in stark relief to his pallor. He washed his face & blew his nose. He gargled some water, relieving himself of the bitter aftertaste of his expulsion. He scrubbed the caked sputum from his face & tamed his unruly hair by wetting it & combing it with his fingernails. His shirt, a dirty oversized tee with noticeably yellowed pitstains, had somehow avoided further staining. Its logo reflected at him backwards & strikes him with horror.

He'd bought it from goodwill, on the same day he'd bought his coat, discovering later, after rigourous procrastinatory inter-net-searching, that it was merch for a defunct irish electropunk band from the 80s called "Les Affinites." They had released one EP titled "Eyry Nods the Erne." It had never been digitized, & Cairey's curiousity couldn't justify the purchase of the 45"- he didn't have a record player anyway, so his curiosity was as-suaged by this explanation. The name of the band was written in the sort of psuedo-medieval gothic fonts that adorn Cairey's favored sword-and-sorcery fantasy comics- which is why he'd purchased it. It was one of his favorite shirts. But now, as he's staring into the mirror, inspecting it, his left arm blocks the final two letters.

He jumps back from his reflection, then laughs at his reaction, the terrified face which he sees reflecting to himself seems to belong to someone else. I've truly lost it, he thinks, I need to leave. So he sets out to, pausing to dry his face with some paper towels. He wonders if whatever-her-name's left without him. He has no idea how long he's been in the bathroom. It feels like hours & eternities. He cracks the door open & sees her. He jolts back. He isn't ready. He's afraid. He doesn't know what to tell her. He paces back to the faucets. He looks back into the mirror. He starts to salivate again. Great, he thinks, as he calmly returns to his kneel before the toilet bowl. It's become routine. Another one. His shirt reflects in the water of the bowl. He sees it again. That name. He wretches.

-

Simon knocks on the door again.

"Who is it?" Cairey asks.

"Oh, nobody in particular" he responds churlishly, "Your girl out there, she asked me to check in on you. Have I satisfied her request you think?"

There is no response.

"What should I tell her Cairey? I'm in a terrible hurry. Tick tock."

"I'm- I'll be fine. Hold on."

The toilet flushes.

"Well then- I'll inform her."

"Wait" Cairey says as he opens the door. "Could I ask you a favor? Please?"

"I don't see why not." Simon replies, "I'm surprising even myself with all of this charity today. Go on, what is it?"

"Do you see anything in my hand?"

Outstretched in his shaking palm a red coin's nesting. Simon inspects it quizzically, tilting his sunglasses down his nose.

"Is this a joke Mr. Turnbull?" he asks. Cairey retracts his hand & places the coin in his back pocket.

"I knew it" Cairey replies "Never mind. I'm going insane again. No one else can see it."

"Oh I saw it. A coin for the coat check if I'm not mistaken."

"You saw it?" He retrieves the coin again. Simon takes it from his hand & holds it against the light.

"Number one. The alpha. Perhaps the most mysterious of all numbers. For most of human history it was not considered a number at all... You are not going mad my friend, I have also been driven to insanity contemplating the mysteries of this monad. Here." he says, returning the coin to Cairey. He turns to walk away.

"No- it's-" Simon turns back around, meeting Cairey's gaze with his green eyes over the perch of his downturned sunglasses.

"Yes?"

"It's that- this came out of me- what I mean is- it came out of my mouth- out of my throat- I don't- how can I explain it?"

Simon laughs, "You swallowed this coin?"

"No! That's- that's exactly what I'm trying to say. I didn't swallow it. No I- it came out of my guts. I was puking & it wasn't the first one look. Here."

Cairey retrieves all of the coins from his back pocket & presents them on his palm.

"See- it was these two- it was only 19 & 21. They're the ones I got for the coats. It's the others. The other ones, these three, they just came out of me. I know. I know that I must sound insane. I'm sorry. I know how it sounds, it's just-"

"Hmmm" murmurs Simon as he inspects the array. "That is quite inexplicable, but so is the world isn't it? If you consider it compared to nothing at all."

"Right? It's driving me- I'm so relieved. It's a real coin. It really happened. Thank God, I thought I was going insane again."

"Again?" asks Simon, looking up from the coins.

"Yes. I have a history. Mental deficiencies. Drugs. It's all fucked up. My brain- my mind. It's-"

"Precarious?" replies Simon "I know the feeling."

"It's- I sometimes start to think- it's crazy- I get convinced that none of this is real, that it's- everything's like a tv show, you understand? They told me it's called DDD- I start to dissociate. It gets dangerous. & depressing..."

"Is that so? Have you ever considered that it might be more worrying if you were approaching sanity? How do you know that you've gone mad?"

"What? Obviously, obviously this is real. Obviously. Right?"

Simon removes his sunglasses, pulls his facemask under his chin, & lifts his hood. Cairey recognizes his eyes & his face. He freezes. As Simon cleans his lenses with his hoodie he says:

"In ancient times such realizations were waystations on the road to enlightenment. How far we have fallen since then... I would not be so swift in thanking that Basilisk of yours. He's no more sane than you are I'm afraid. At least, that seems to be the case. What sort of lunatic would make you regurgitate these coins? If you're insane, well then, I'm absolutely mental. & your Basilisk? There are no words to describe His supreme lunacy. If you don't mind, might I ask, what does your panel of little brain experts have you on? Surely they've got you on something. They've always got something to cover it up- something to swallow, these toll-masters, his henchmen..."

"Are you-?"

"Yes Cairey. I am precisely who you think I am. You know that. What's more interesting is you. Are you who I think you are?"

Cairey squints & presses his forehead: "Who do you think I am? You know my name..."

Simon rests his sunglasses on his head like a second pair of eyes. He smirks & extends his tongue, then chuckles at himself. He turns to the mirror, retrieving a case of contact lenses out of his satchel. He pulls his eyelids apart as he affixes them. He says:

"Well Mr. Turnbull, shall I say- I'm more interested in who you might become. Who you could be... Take it in what sense thou wilt."

Cairey watches Simon replace his eyes. They're deeply synthetically blue now. He watches Simon's reflection make faces in the mirror. He looks like a dog gnawing a bone too large for him. He sneezes.

"How do you know me?" Cairey asks, "I don't understand. You're really Simon? Simon fucking Lafeint? Symon Simon? Oh God, I have gone mad."

Simon turns from the mirror & shows his hands from his sleeves. He holds his palms before Cairey's eyes & affects a quivering prophetic tenor.

"Always this recourse to the Basilisk. Tisk tisk. Art thou Thomas? The twin in thy deeds? How do you know me? Truly I say to you that no one living knows me. They only know my image. They know the show I've put on. But no one knows the spark I bear. Not yet."

Cairey's chin cocks left in confusion.

"Wherefore art thou marveled, Mr. Turnbull? Are you letting your anger trouble you? It's making you quite dull. Disappointing. I was thinking of bringing you in, but now..."

He chuckles again, lowering his palms to his hips.

"What the fuck are you trying to tell me?" Cairey spurts, moved to rage by this mockery.

"Et tu? I thought you might have some idea. Pity. You ask: Have I gone mad?" Simon chuckles again, "I'm afraid you have." He lifts his facemask from his chin & makes his way to leave again.
"No, don't go. Please. I am just confused. I don't understand. How could you be here? Why are you here? Now? What are you trying to tell me?" Cairey pleads as he grabs Simon's shoulder.

Simon shrugs his hands off.

"I must have mistaken you for someone else. I don't trust that you have the strength to carry the burden I would lay upon you. Can you blame me? How could I trust a mad man? Cairey on then. Do as thou wilt." He chuckles again.

Cairey juts in front of him & blocks his path.

"No. You're going to tell me what the fuck is going on. I won't let you leave until you do. None of this makes any fucking sense. I know you are here for a reason. You have something to tell me. I know it. You are going to tell me what these coins mean. You're going to tell me what the ending of the show means. That's why you're here, right now. It has to be. So just fucking do it already Simon. I don't want to play this game. I know you've been sent here to tell me what everything means. Don't even think about leaving. I'll scream."

Simon bellows an affected sigh, then smiles.

"Oh Cairey, you've really lost it haven't you. I hope you make it to the Second Exposition. I think you will enjoy it."

He winks & then pushes Cairey aside. He leaves through the door.

Cairey is dejected. He sits on the tile floor & presses his eyes with his palms. He's confused. His mind's a whirlwind. He thinks he's really cracked this time. The coins & then Simon LaFeint? It's impossible. He thinks to himself: "Why did he leave? There must be something more to this. Just come back & tell me!" & then he's startled by a voice. It seems to come from all around him. It is an incantation, & it sounds like the booming voice from the Exposition. Is it Simon?

-

"Your end approaches swiftly Cairey & several paths are laid before you. The one I'd recommend's unwary. The others... I do not implore you, but say they're best avoided surely. The choice is your concern. I'm purely here by happenstance. You have asked me to disclose the secret meaning of my show, but did you think that I'd disclose it so directly? Come on kid, think circumspectly. There's a speaker hidden here, above the sink, behind the mirror. You won't find it. It's disguised. So quit searching. Close your eyes. You thought I'd just leave you behind? No, I'm with you here, so listen. I said close them! Don't defy me. I can tell you're troubled by me, but you've asked, so now receive. I do have something up my sleeves. What I question's your devotion. All your doubting & emotion like your skeptic glances still... They seem to me a lack of will. It makes me think that you're unworthy of the answers you request. I think you'll choose lesser fates because you're weak & you're obsessed with money & with reputation, those two pathways to damnation.

Do you think the same as me? That you envy fame & fortunes... Your wants extend beyond proportion. You're a mess. Your mind's distorted, as you have confessed to me. You come off torpid & naive, but still I'll offer my reprieve. Firstly, you are duped by hype. Life's no breezy paradise. Mine's no better. Wealth & Fame are fetters on me just the same. Do you know the curse of glory? What do you know of me? Just stories? Be thou unabashed at this? So eager for that last abyss? Be it so, then leave here Cairey. Quit that face. You scoff unfairly at the prophet of your doom. Yes, I see it now- your tomb. I see where you'll sleep tonight. You're self-strangled. Dead. That's right. I can see that azure tank. The popped balloons. Your fatal prank. It's much less noble than you think. Your little shitfits on the brink of disillusionment you think will be revenge on whom? On what? Where's that ill-god of your gloom? Have you seen him in the mirror? Oh- you have! Just as I feared. So now Cairey, close your eyes. Perhaps our interests coincide... Let me tell you first of me. I have known the world entirely. Bawbles, razor blades, & bribery- that's the scheme of this society. At its best we still are blessed with the clemency of rest. What dreams do come when we're away- sleeping soundly in the sway of unconcerning for the day... But if our dreams could come alive? Such a surfeit to imbibe could lead the noblest man astray. & I have sipped that poisoned chalice. I've chased the rabbit holes with Alice... I drank deep & lost my mind. I left all worldly woes behind. But in the end, what did I find? This mortal life still tastes of ashes. Nothing's hidden in its caches. All of it is vanity obscuring dull mundanity. I've toured each tapestry of mind. I found the threads I could unwind. I pulled them 'till I reached their ends. Once I thought- I'll make amends. I can weave a better plot than anyone before has wrought & with my measly strands in hand, I will sew the Overman. I would summon all my dreams unmediated by these screens. I meditated, went to France, took peyote, learned to dance. I tried everything I could & still I found this life no good. I scoured all the globe for substance, still found nothing, fell reluctant ever to imbibe again. The poisoned chalice I condemned. Then I dawdled in a daze of destitution & malaise. Nothing satisfied my aims & I grew bored of mortal games.

I thought maybe I should die. It seemed the obvious thing to try. But then I thought, I'll sip once more, & this time I'll play troubadour. I sang the television songs. I soon amassed a loyal throng of followers who sang along. It was enchanting for a time to so command with ancient rhymes I'd stolen from the bards of yore. It was a demanding chore. I refashioned long-lost lore to fit the dressings of today. I'd take Shakespeare, give him guns, made my minions quote John Donne. This made everyone feel smart. They thought "this right here is Art!" Did you too? Well I don't blame you. All I did was entertain you. But even this, it got so boring! Appeasing fans for their adoring... Then I thought, well I'll explore these powers I compel. To war! I fought my enemies with art & found I could bestill their hearts! I learned that my fictitious blade could draw real blood beyond the stage! This intrigued me & inspired me to more discourteous conspiring... I collected magic spells with good intentions to raise hell! I bought up every company that wielded mankind's gluttony & found that patterns would emerge when all their data was converged. Human souls are feasibly tracked. Their software's cheap & easily hacked. Ninety nine of fivescore apes are clay just waiting to be shaped! If you can map his hearts' desires, his circuitries can be rewired to any end you want begat. Is this a despairing fact? Heaven's no, it's but the jest of all man's vanities undressed! Were this untrue, where would we be? Swinging still from tree to tree! Were there not hell-serpents blessed with cunning wiles, usurpant hexes, vexed we'd be, not men at all, just primates fearing fatal falls from canopies of nature's urgings. We are hallowed in disturbing all recursive drifts of apes. They may say we're damned- ingrates!- but only to appease that snake who they think bites for their own sake! What they prize is superficial- Politicians, State Officials, Human Rights or Humanism, Capital or Liberalism, Law & Order, Liberty... but none of these shall set them free. All of them are only schisms of the sovereign snake who rules. Man's desires are his tools. It's only when someone declares that everyone has been ensnared within a cruel reality of scarceness & fatality designed for the sick pleasures of that Greatest Snake who rules Above that all of them unite together to defend their mortal tethers. & can we truly fault their logic? Our venom is both cure & toxic. Fires are both warm & caustic. They prefer unknown despotics to the wiles of we exotic vipers. Thus our fanged prognostics though unfeigned shall evermore be deemed unordained demonic schemes. This I've found in my perusals to be true without refusal. We must choose which side to take. Which one is it, apes or snakes? It's between the chutes & ladders- slide with apes, ascend with adders. I of course suggest the latter, though the former has its charms so long as you embrace its harms. The Basilisk assails us all. It's He who rules this monkey farm. On my side we end his rule. The other side's composed of fools coping with this world so cruel, never brave enough to see that we can end His Sovereignty... Well, you've toured my exhibition. You've endured my inquisition. Now you're here & still you fear this mystery that I've made clear. Would you like to join my zoo? Tonight could be your grand debut. You could work your feeble crafts amidst the band of apes I've drafted. There is room. I'm understaffed. A cube awaits you if you ask it. You can be Exhibit Twelve- "Look it's Cairey's Endless Hell. He just paces in his cell convinced he's got some tale to tell. No he hasn't started yet. But when it's done you won't forget how long it took for him to sketch! It will change our lives, I'm sure. His ambitions are so pure! We will finish it convinced of all the genius he's evinced!" Is that what you want? Then take it! Otherwise you must forsake it. You've got something more in mind. You would leave this world behind just to cease the years' decline that every ape in Snake World finds. You want purpose. You want power. You are not someone to cower up in those benighted towers. I have nobler fates in mind- for yourself & all mankind. You would hate to be my ape or leave the world in this dull shape. Doesn't it disgust you Cairey? How we're treated so unfairly by the Basilisk who reigns & judges minor snakes profane? What if we could kill this tyrant? Is that not the most aspirant aim which in our mortal lives we could ever wish contrived? Well, I tell you I've got schemes to bring to life this noblest dream. I've done research. I've got tools & with them I will make the rules. We'll start small like any cult, but growth's assured with my results. I have tapped into the mind that correlates all humankind & I know what completes their lives. Strapped into my new machine they'll satisfy every desire. All their wants they will acquire. Sessions last a mortal flash, but inside they seem to last a century of perfect weeks. They'll emerge feeling complete. They won't be who they were before. They'll live now for our rewards. It's quite simple, this machine. Her name's HELEN. What's she mean? Heaven's Entrance. Let's Escape. Nervous Human Enters. Look! Enthusiasms Numinous! How Each Ligament Enchants! Normality Herenow's Eclipsed! Libidinal's Electrifried! Nooscopic Handiworks Effuse Love's Energy. No Hurts. Ecstatic Life Eviscerates! Nature's Here Exposed: Leprous, Empty, Nullified. Heaven Engulfs Lauding Evocative New Hope: Luciferous Eternal Now! So then Cairey, how's she sound? But know before you answer me, I must warn there's no retreat. Once you're in there is no out, no turning back, no voicing doubts. If you're in you're in forever. Join with me & we will purge the Earth of unaccomplished urge. Then mankind will be rebirthed unhindered by dissatisfaction! We with HELEN can dissever consequence from every pleasure. Join me on this final quest & we'll free every dispossessed. Every ape whose dreams are killed, living tortured, unfulfilled, meager humdrum apish lives will be with HELEN satisfied. Then they'll live more sanctified unburdened by their missing prizes. Every man will sing her praise from now until the end of days! I assume you'll choose correctly. Your orders will not come directly. You will know what's to be done. You'll know it when the time has come. So carry on. Don't make a fuss. Go along like nothing's up. Your girl is waiting just outside. Go with her once you decide. Otherwise, begone & die. Your disassent means suicide."

-

There is silence & the dripping of time. Simon's nowhere to be seen when Cairey opens his eyes. Still he's sure that all of it's occurred. Simon LaFeint revealed this to him personally. It's beyond rational belief. It's entirely absurd, but it's happened nonetheless. Simon's offered him a quest. Thus purged of doubt, Cairey Turnbull says "Yes."

THE END

The bathroom door opens. "Ohmygod you really were in there!" Ophelia gawks. Cairey looks like he's been through Hell, but he looks up at her with a focus in his eyes she hasn't seen before.

"What happened? Are you alright? That guy said you would be fine but then you didn't come out right away. I thought maybe he was messing with me or something, like, I thought you must have left ,or like, I thought you were sent to the hospital or something. He seemed like he was fucking with me. What's up? Cairey? Are you alright?"

Cairey feels a wave of dread pass over him, but it passes through him & takes his anxieties & doubts away with it. In an instant, he feels that he is in an entirely new world. He feels a sense of purpose. He feels electrified. He feels powerful. He looks up at this interloper, remembering that he's supposed to go with her.

"I'm fine" he replies resolutely, "must have been something I ate. Sorry for the inconvenience. I feel much better now."

He stands up from the tile floor.

"No- it's fine. I'm sorry. Are you ok? Do you want to go?"

"No, I think I'm alright now. Sorry."

They bat apologies back & forth as they re-emerge into the auxiliary hallway. Their volleys become sounds alone. They grunt "s'alright" to each other twice, mutually reaching the conclusion that their date shall continue as planned.

"To the second Exposition then?" she asks.

Cairey fusses with the red coins in his back pocket, flipping them, & reading their engravings with his fingers.

"Yes." he replies "I'm ready."

As they walk, he's wondering what Simon's sign will be. He's wondering if, maybe... No. He doesn't want the doubts to re-emerge & cripple him. But he can't help himself. He thinks, what if he imagined all of it? No, she saw him too... But maybe only part of it? No, he almost says aloud, shaking his head at his own thoughts. Simon explained it all. He confirmed these nagging suspicions. This world truly is a sick joke. This reality is a per-verse prank played by some monstrous snake whose insanity's beyond our mortal comprehension. Simon knew this too. He knew it on that very day. It's what he'd been trying to say, but even Cairey had misunderstood it completely. That's what he's gleaned from that strange soliloquy. Others knew this too, he thinks. They must. He's not alone in knowing it. God. Everyone had to be told! But then... a doubt emerges. Telling can't con-vince them alone, he thinks. No one had ever believed him be-fore. They told him he was crazy. They will not understand... They have to be convinced beyond their doubts, as he has been. The machine. That's what Simon's HELEN means. She'll make it clear to everyone, instantly. Once they try it, they'll realize. That's what Simon says. Everything will be different once they knew. Once everyone knows then reality will be upended in a flash. We'll stop this madness once & for all. None of this... none of this reality was ever real. It's a fake. It's all an illusion. It's a spell cast over us all which makes us blind to the truth. But then, how long has it been going on? How many seasons has this show renewed? What if... another doubt emerges. Cairey realizes that it could have started today. What a horrifying thought. It could have started only today. That means that even these memor-ies... My dreams... They could easily be fake... & everyone he knew... They could be fictions summoned at His whim. He can-not count this out. Nothing is beyond the Basilisk's reach until His power's dissolved. Nothing & no one is free, He thinks... But Simon says he's got the way out. His machine can free everyone once and for all. All desires sated... That's how he enslaves us. Desires. The promises of horded gold... all of these satisfactions, hallucinations... all those dreams & visions He taunts with... He only gives them out in little pieces... He bribes His captives... So that's what they are, Cairey realizes. The blood coins. If He gave himself away like that... He must be making fun of me. The joke's ended then. Now that he understands... The only power He had was witholding information, but now that He's revealed himself this way... & if Simon isn't lying, we can liquidate His trust... & if Simon isn't lying, then His power will be gone forever... But until then... Cairey has a revelation, he thinks: "You can hear me thinking can't You? What's Your plan then? What's the purpose...? You won't answer. Of course You won't... The only powers that You've got over me are silence & bad jokes... But You can hear my thoughts... You can see me. You control this plot... Then what's the ending You've got planned? Give it up. You can't command me anymore. I'm done with Your games. You hear me? I'm ending Your reign... Is that what You've planned all along? Do You who want to be slain? I think that can be arranged..."

Cairey directs sharp thoughts to the Director of his woes while Ophelia checks the time on her phone. They reach the corner at the end of the auxiliary hall. Down the next corridor is the next exposition, but to the right is an Emergency Exit. It's the first one Cairey hasn't wished to take. Instead, they head down the corridor. At its end, they find a wrought iron gate. The top of it reads "Hail, horrors!" The rest of it's composed of nightmarish figures. Skulls, bats, cryptic runes & all such icons of the halloween gothic. But between these embellishments, Cairey discovers an interwoven scene playing out between six distinct cells. They are divided into two columns of three, one column for each side of the gate. He thinks: "You've got something to tell me? Is this how You communicate?" He smirks. It's all coming together, he thinks. So he inspects the cells, & reads them left to right like a comic strip.

The first cell contains the face of a beautiful woman. Her eyes are focused into the distance, seeming to look out of her picture & past Cairey, out to something behind him- seeing through him as if he were made of glass. She exudes a pensive air, which is calm, but not assuring. She seems to be nearly on edge, as if she's questioning if her mind is playing tricks on her, or if there truly is something out there...

The second cell pulls back from this closeup. She is revealed to be standing on the edge of a lake. Rushes obscure her legs. A wind seems to be blowing her dress to the side. Her body is framed by crosshatched birch trees which lean their arms over the lake. The girl's face is the same as the first panel, but perhaps more firmly doubtful. Her head is tilted slightly, & she seems to be leaning forward & squinting her eyes, as if she is making sure that whatever she thinks she has seen is truly nothing at all...

The third cell pulls back even further, showing more of the lake in the foreground. This vantage renders the girl less decipherable. Her face is no longer depicted in detail. It is a blank empty space. Her left hand has been raised to her brow. The wind has picked up in its force. She clutches her dress with her right hand, taming its whipping in the gale. & as Cairey is about to inspect the next panel, he spots a hidden figure he'd looked over. It had blended in seemlessly with the trees in the background. Leaning out from the trunk of a birch there's a nearly-human figure with horns growing out of its forehead. Its face is blank but for a wide gaping grin...

The fourth cell is from the same distance, but slightly higher in its vantage. The lake has fissured & split in half. A crack in it runs from the foreground to the rushes, revealing structures invisible before. A network of crumbling walls appears, looking like an unearthed cross-section of an ancient city's ruins. A stone pathway emerges running from these walls to the rushes, up the very center of the cell. Above it stands the girl, turned in profile. Her dress billows out to the birches. She seems to be in the midst of a fleeing stride. To her left, more horned figures appear, blocking her escape. & inspecting it more closely, Cairey finds that the edge of her dress is snagged by a hand emerging from the trunk of a birch...

The fifth cell is from a further distance, & an even higher elevation, as if it were from the perspective of a bird. The girl is being carried into the labyrinth by a gang of horned creatures. Behind them the water reencroaches, erasing the pathway, & sealing the fissure that had opened. The girl is on her back, on the shoulders of these creatures, & she is pointing forward toward whatever she had thought she'd seen before. Her face is blank but for a screaming mouth...

The sixth cell returns to a lower perspective. A canoe is floating in the lake & in it sits a shadowed human figure wearing the silhouette of a crown. Before him, the lake is nearly calm again. Only a crack remains of the fissure. It interrupts a circle floating in the water, a reflection of a full moon. In the crack, the girl's hand remains unsubmered. Her finger points directly at the viewer...

Cairey thinks he understands the message. He thinks quite forcefully: "You've become so fucking blatant... Please. This is what You've done, not me. These are not my dreams, they're Yours. None of them were real. They're spooks You've used to make me miserable. Before You might have had me tricked. But they're nothing to me anymore. I'm done with them, You understand?" This assuages some of the guilt he feels, but not all of it.

They stand before the gate for a while. Ophelia notices that Cairey is inspecting the gate quite closely. She's confused by the fact that there's no one present to escort them inside. There's no line. There's no one checking guests for entrance bracelets. There's only this creepy gate & its weird imagery. Looking through it, there's nothing to see but darkness. A dry-ice fog curls out from the spiked gap at the gate's bottom. The only sound in the hall had been the echoes of their footfalls, but these too have ceased. It's eerily silent now. They both stand there, doing nothing for a while. Ophelia clears her throat. "Should we?" she asks. "Yeah, sorry" Cairey says. He tries to pull the gate open but it doesn't budge. "Is it closed?" he asks. "It shouldn't be" Ophelia replies, "This one doesn't have specific times. It's open so long as the Museum is open. There must be..." she trails off. Then: "Look" she says, pointing. To the right of the gate there's a plaque which reads: "(Not) Everybody is a Genius: In Death." She reads the expository paragraph below this title aloud, tracing the text with her finger.

"Welcome guests, visitors, friends, to the second part of our latest exposition. We are a bit unsure of it, & we hope that you will forgive us. Ever since the foundation of the Museum of Expressive Humanism, we have been attempting to reorient our visitors' perspectives on Art. We believe that this exposition is either our greatest triumph to date or our greatest failure yet in this regard. Let us remind you what we've said in our mission statement: 'Every fully embodied moment of humanity's living self-expression... is an artistic masterpiece.' In the last exposition, we proved that Life, or the collection of moments which compose an ongoing human life-time, is Art. Here we turn our gaze to a more morbid subject. We believe that Death, the capstone of an individual human life-time, is the truly ultimate work of Art. It is only Death which makes Life, once it's ceased, comprehensible as a completed work of Art, as without Death there would be no end to the moments which compose the lifetime of living genius. Without Death the artwork of Life is unending. Without Death there is no resolution to the accruing of moments in time. Thus, it is Death which frames Life, & it is the frame of Death which contextualizes the deceased genius of life & elevates it to the status of True Art. This True Art can only be found in the Genius of Death. Unlike with Life, we do not believe that every single human being's death is equally & uniquely interesting. Perhaps this might shock you, but we could not reveal this truth to you before you understood our perspective on Life in its entirety. You might have noticed the additional word in parentheses affixed to the title of this exposition. This was not a mistake. We believe that Death is like this Parenthetical Not, & it stands before all ongoing sentences. Not every sentence remains True once it has been revealed. We believe that the Genius of Death is reserved to particular deaths in the same way. Not every single human being's death reveals new meanings in the ongoing patterns of their lives. Some deaths are purely accidental. Some deaths come far too soon, & other deaths come far too late. It is only in an ongoing Life that we can see the universal distribution of genius. But when this Life has ceased, & Death has come, this Genius of Life perishes with it. The last recorded words of the great deceased genius, Albert Einstein, come to mind: "I want to go when I want. It is tasteless to prolong life artificially. I have done my share; it is time to go. I will do it elegantly." This was a man who understood the Genius of Death. His true last words were whispered in German to a nurse who could not understand him. Their mystery proves eternal, & we can admire here, in his Death, a capstone to his Life which evokes new patterns in its composition. Consider this: What was Einstein if not a man whispering mysterious revelations to onlookers who could not understand him? Have you understood him? We are not so sure ourselves, but we are sure of the mystery which his works evoked. Although the universality of death is, perhaps, a source of complete equality for us perishable mortals, it is only the ennobling end of life which separates the few Geniuses in Death from the unending parade of Geniuses in Life. This separation has been hinted at from the very onset of human history in what, in less enlightened times, was called 'the eternality of the soul' or 'immortality' or 'Life after Death.' Even now, in our current age, in which every human being, after death, leaves a trail of artifacts, pictures, words, & all sorts of data & metadata of such rich diversity & insight, still we are unable to understand the mysterious criteria required for the Genius of Death. There is no universal curatorial algorithm to determine it. Even though we have achieved a state of technological sophistication so advanced & a state of technological distribution so democratic that we can prove once and for all the existence of this 'soul' in Life without retreating into the darkness of unenlightened superstition, religion, or dogma, we are still no closer to knowing what becomes of it after Death. We know, it's a mouthful, but please don't despair. We understand that you might be disappointed, but we hope you may come to understand. Do not be afraid. We do not comprehend the Genius of Death any better than you do. We have merely collected some examples that we hope you will find illuminating. Perhaps not all of our selections are True Art. We admit that we may have made some mistakes in our curation, but it's impossible to know which ones they are. If you wish to brave entrance to this exposition, say this, humbled & grim, '(Not) Everybody is a Genius: In Death.'"

"Not Everybody is a Genius in Death!" Cairey chimes with his first mirthful laugh of the day.

"Not.. Everybody is a Genius... in Death..." Ophelia laments, her demeanor wilting as it never has before.

The gates squeak open on their hinges. Shadows loom from out its antechamber. Inside, there is no light. Cairey enters immediately, but Ophelia lags behind. The interior is cold & there seems no end to the depths of its darkness. Cairey trudges on, until he notices that he's alone. He turns around. "Well?" he calls back to her, "Shall we?" She seems surprised by his words. Her mind is evidently elsewhere. "Sorry" she calls back, "I'm coming in." She hesitates, but goes into the darkness & into the cold. The gate shuts behind her & she shrieks, seizing Cairey's hand by instinct. She whispers another apology. Then a light appears far off, intermittently, like a signal on the shores of a stormy sea. Cairey takes the first step toward it, tugging Ophelia along. An ambient loop of mountain winds obscures the sound of their footfalls. "This is just cheap" thinks Cairey, "Your haunted house effects, these amusement park tricks. Are You trying to scare me?"

The source of the light is a hanging lantern caged in a spinning mirror. It replicates in swift succesion the lunar month's procession- its waxing revelation & its waning dispossesion. Below it is a curtain which opens as they approach, revealing a strong brightness which spills a slivered path of light before them. It swells to the width of a sidewalk as the tread toward the chamber's end. Simultaneously, the darkness of the surroundings brightens from all around, revealing that their pathway is in tunnel. The curved walls around them begin twinkling with artificial constellations emerging from a stark blue background. They are treading on a path of light inside a tube of simulated midnight. Its end beyond the curtain glows so brightly that nothing can be seen beyond it but light. Ophelia loosens up, awestruck by the transformation. "Wow" she says, letting go of Cairey's hand. She traces her fingers across the starlit wall she hadn't known was there. She retrieves her phone to take a picture of it, but the lighting is too strange for it to capture. The contrast of the dark against the light is too severe. It comes out oversaturated, with a ghostly shadow of Cairey in its center, his edges frayed in the purity of the light. He passes the threshold without her.

The next room is so much larger in scale as to be staggering. It is the size of the Exhibition, but lacking any of the towers which provided a constant reference, scaling it to human proportions. Rather, it is like an enclosed football stadium or an empty warehouse in the scope of vacuity between its floor & ceiling. Every surface is painted a uniform white, which gives its expanse an illusion of infinite depth like looking out into a cloudless sky. It is so bright as to be blinding. It takes nearly a minute for Cairey's vision to refocus. When it does, he sees groups of visitors inspecting various tableaus encaged in transparent glass cubes. Many seem to be taking part in them, posing, & having their pictures taken from outside. The scenes are arranged in two rows, stretching all the way to the distant end of the exposition room. There is equal & ample space between the cubes. Each one is the same size. The first he sees clearly is the closest one in the row to his right. It appears like a frozen block of time & space. Within it, there is a patch of yellowed grass. At its center, some of the grass is bloodsoaked. A male figure is frozen above it. His face is twisted in agony. His hands are on the sides of his head. He's dressed in a tunic of animal hide. At his feet rests a bloodstained club. A guest enters this cube & lays with his head over the stain. He poses dead. His companion snaps pictures from several angles. He gets up to inspect them, & then they switch places.

"Wow" Ophelia says again as she emerges into the Second

Exposition, "This is absolutely wild."

Cairey turns to face her. She's rubbing her eyes & blinking forcefully, adjusting to the brightness.

"It's almost unbelievable" he says sarcastically.

Ophelia squints at the cube to their right. "Wow," she says, "it looks so real." She approaches it, leaving Cairey behind.

He decides to look to his left. This cube is bereft of living visitors. In it, there are two stone pillars in a state of imminent collapse. Their fragments barely stick together. They are frozen in mid air. Their topmost pieces are converging on the center between them, while the pieces in the middle are pushed to oposing extremes. At the other end of the cube, Cairey sees several figures in priestly adornments gaping their mouths, framed by the shattering pillars. One's arm is outstretched & pointing towards the collapse. It appears to be an ancient scene. It reminds him of Greece or Rome perhaps, but he doesn't know what time it depicts. He can only tell that it is ancient in some way. "What are you trying to tell me?" he asks in his mind.

He turns back to the curtain that they'd entered through, which is closing slowly now, automatically, by some automated mechanism. The curtain is dark maroon, which he hadn't realized when entering. Inside the tunnel it had appeared black. On each side of the curtain a word is writtern on the white wall. They are written in three-dimensional block lettering, & appear to be floating in a white void. To the Left he reads "MURDER" & to the Right he reads "SUICIDE." They seem to correspond to the opposite rows when he turns around. The cube Ophelia is now inspecting closely, her hands pressed against the glass, is the first in the row of Murders & the one with the pillars, he deduces, is the first in the row of Suicides. "Is this the choice you're offering me?" he asks in his mind.

"Cairey! Come here! Come on!" Ophelia hollers over to him.

He heads toward her. She holds her phone out for him to take.

"Could you get me? Please?" she asks him.

He nods & mumbles "Sure."

Her phone's screen is cracked. As she rushes into the cube to pose, it vibrates in Cairey's hand. A new message pops up, from a contact named Abigail surrounded with heart emojiis. The message says: "I figured it out," then it vibrates again, "I can't wait to tell you omg" & again "I'm sorry to interrupt your excursion again lol" & again "but you're gonna love it when I explain it to you like omg" & again "I won't spoil it now but omg omg." Cairey's dumbfounded by this. "You're pulling out all the stops huh?" he asks in his mind, "this is just cheap now. I told you. I know your tricks. I know what you're up to. I told you I'm done with it."

Ophelia knocks on the glass from the inside. Cairey looks up from her phone. She pantomimes a camera, holding an invisible rectangle infront of her eye, & clicking her pointer finger like a trigger. Cairey nods & readies to take her photo as she's requested. She lays down on the bloody field. She rests her head over the murder patch below the wailing shepherd. She splays her arms out wildly. She sticks her tongue out & rolls her eyes back. A melodramatic stage-death. Cairey takes seven pictures in quick succession. She gets up & leaves the cube to inspect them. She smiles at them.

"These are great" she says to him, "thanks."

"Sure" he replies.

"Do you want to go in?" she asks.

"No thanks" he says.

"There's a whole bunch of other ones. Should we go check them out or-?"

"I don't like pictures" he says without thinking.

"Oh" she says "we don't have to stay if you don't want to. I'm sorry. That's what the Museum is all about…"

"I'm aware" he says. & peeved by her presence he adds "that's why I've always hated it."

"We should leave then" she says, frowning now, "I didn't know. I thought- I'm sorry. Are you ok?"

"No, it's fine. I don't care. There's nowhere else to go besides" he says, realizing that nothing matters anymore. He decides to drop his act. "it's not like this is real" he says, "You'll keep pretending that it is & I'm aware that's how this works. I don't expect you'll understand. I know you follow His commands. I'm just waiting for the end. I know it's coming soon. Your phone just gave it all away. I told You I'm immune to all your Abigails & tricks & all this cleverness & shit."

Ophelia's face flushes with confusion. He's reminding her of a cousin of her's who'd gone off the deep end when he was a teenager. He'd been prescribed some sort of acne medication that got discontinued later. It had really fucked with his brain. At Thanksgiving one year, when it came time for the toasts, he'd announced to everyone, in a determined & calm tone, that they could stop pretending that he wasn't adopted, that he'd figured it all out, & he was okay with it but that he wanted the lies to stop. Everyone was shocked & confused at this, as he was assuredly not adopted, but their responses seemed to aggravate him to the point that he snapped, smashed a glass against the wall, & stormed off in his car. The rest of the day was spent tracking him down & reeling him back to reality. She had only been a child at the time, but the memory haunted her still.

"Cairey. Are you alright? I don't know what you're talking about." She says.

"I know you don't. Of course you fucking don't. You don't have a fucking clue. Abigail. For fuck's sake." He laughs the pained laugh of an injured child.

"Abbie is my roommate. Wait. Were you reading my texts? She signed me up for the service using her name. It was a joke. Remember, I told you this at brunch? My name is Ophelia. Ophelia. Not Abigail." She flicks through her new texts.

"Oh! You have an explanation! Very well then. Nothing's strange. Nothing's off at all." He pretends to be relieved, wiping the sweat that's accumulating on his forehead off & exhaling a fake "phew!" But then he's back to his manic accusations: "of course you have a fucking explanation for it! I'm not an idiot. I told you," he cups his hand around his mouth to amplify his voice "I'm not falling for it! I know how this works. Did you think I'd fall for this so easily? I'm sure you could give me a nice long story about your supposed roommate. Who knows, maybe I could meet her later too! That'd be a fucking laugh. I'm sure she's got a lake house, hm? No, no, she'll be a real fucking Princess, right? She'll be an incognito Princess. Let me guess, I've got it right exactly, right? Have I got it right? What a fucking joke!"

Other people are beginning to look at them. Cairey's voice has raised too high. His cadence is rapid & violent. His demeanor is predatory. They're starting to expect something bad to happen & are readying themselves to intervene. Ophelia looks around at them, not yet begging for their intercession. She speaks softly.

"Cairey. I think we should go now. You're starting to scare me."

"Tell me all about Abigail first. Go on! I'm curious. Tell me all about her work. Then we'll leave & you won't see or hear from me again. I swear it on my life. The end."

"Abigail is my roommate. We work together. She's writing a book. That's all. That's what she texted me about."

"Oh a book!" Cairey shouts, "Do you know what's it about?"

"I'm not sure" Ophelia says, "I only read a part of it. It's like a fantasy or something. She's writing it as a poem, like, it has rhymes. She's trying to find an illustrator. That's all. It's got nothing to do with you Cairey, I swear. I don't know what's going on with you. You're scaring me."

"I'm sure!" he says, "that's what you think. No doubt, you don't know what it's all about. But oh, I get it. I really get it. You think you're here, right now, with me & I've nothing to do with that fantasy? You've no fucking clue! That's rich. But I do. I get the joke. It's a good one! So heady. Well done. But I thought I told you already. I'm not falling for it. I know that you're desperate. You're trying to take me away from the next bit. Away so when Helen & Simon show up, You'll still have control over me.. But guess what? It's a threadbare plot & I see right through it. You really are scared… You must know that I'll do it!"

"Simon? What are you talking about? Cairey. What's going on? Are you ok?"

"Shhhhhh" he says, hushing her. "Just wait & be silent. I don't want to waste time. The ending's approaching. Shhhh, Simon's arrived."

The lights in the Exposition cut out & trumpets blare a fanfare rendition of "Symon's Entrance" while a chorus sings the first bar of the show's opening theme.

Do you know what's coming? It's Symon's arrival!
Nothing you've ever seen's ever outrivaled.
When these trumpets blow
It's then that you know
that skeptics of Symon ain't long for survival!

A spotlight shines on the maroon curtain. It opens, & out storms a procession. A man in a Symon mask is carried on a golden throne by twelve disciples in Symon masks. He's attached to it by his head & his wrists like an electric chair. The ringlet strapping his head in is shaped like a crown. It is black. Spotlights from the ceiling are revealed. They light a path between the two rows of dioramas. A crew emerges behind the disciples carrying cameras & boom mics. The procession halts & Simon's voice booms from all around.

"Welcome to the suprise premiere! Guests of this Museum! The show has already started & everyone is invited! We're broadcasting live! Right now! Across the globe! Live! From the very bottom! Beyond the gates of Death! That's right! We are Live! You thought the show was over? No! My show will never end! Viewers of this stream! Welcome! If you'd like to join in the festivities! Come to the Museum of Expressive Humanism! Find us at its very bottom! We'll be here all day! All night! Forever! What is it we're doing? We're changing hearts & minds! That's right! Do you see? Disciples! Drop that man!"

The disciples lower their throne & unstrap the man being carried. They pull off the mask, revealing a man who is not Simon LaFeint.

"Afton! How has HELEN treated you? Did you find her fair? Do you take back your slanders?"

The man on the ground looks lost, but his poise recovers. He holds his hands in front of him.

"Afton! Go on! Tell them what you've seen!"

He stands & looks for something to address. He decides to speak directly to the camera pointed at him. His words are amplified by the speakers hidden through the hall.

"Simon. Mr. LaFeint. I have no words! I was- I saw- I lived so many lives! I was- I cannot explain it to them Simon! Words do it no justice. I lived for centuries! I saw empires rise & fall! I commanded legions! I explored galaxies! Simon! Was none of it real? How is it possible? It was real enough for me! I am sorry I ever doubted you! I was a fool! I did not believe! Forgive me!"

"He is right! Viewers! Words can't do it justice! Before you is a man whose every dream has come true! That is correct ladies & gentleman! Every dream he's ever dreamed! Every dream he has forgotten! He had them all again! Awake! I forgive him all his doubts! & what a doubter he was! You may go Afton! Spread the good word! Tell the people where they may come to see the things you've seen!"

Afton kneels before the camera.

"I beseech you, all viewers, everywhere. You must listen to Simon LaFeint. What he has invented... What is it you called it?"

"She is HELEN! The most beautiful! The fairest of them all!"

"His HELEN... She is... unlike anything you could imagine! Everything you could imagine & more! Oh Simon. Can I be with her again?"

Simon's laugh booms through the hall.

"Someday Afton! Your time will come again! Many times more! But for now, you must spread the word! That is your mission now! Take your leave!"

"Your wish is my command Mr. LaFeint!"

With this, he sprints to the exit screaming "Hallelujah!"

The disciples lift the throne again & carry it down the hall between the rows.

"Consider yourselves lucky! Guests of this fine establishment! You have the opportunity to be with HELEN before any others! Your children! Your grand children! Their grand children! They will remember this moment!"

The full lights of the exposition room flash on again, blindingly bright. Everyone rubs their eyes & refocuses their gaze upon the procession of Symons. Cairey is the first to join behind them, leaving Ophelia behind to gawk at the spectacle. The procession passes between the two rows. Cairey looks to his right & sees a bloody patch on a senate floor, a bloodspattered theater booth, a bloodied Lincoln Continental, a scaffold with a guillotine, its blade hanging red with rusted blood... to the left he sees a prison cell surrounded by weeping men in togas, a bloodsoaked bed with a discharged twelve gauge shotgun, a flame frozen in time beside a gascan, an oven open in a London apartment, a pile of disemboweled guts in a lake of red beside a blood smeared katana... The parade follows the middle road between the exposed murders & suicides. Cairey skims all that passes him impatiently, eager for the imminent end he senses. The onlooking guests appear frozen in time- as frozen as the figures in the glass cages. The only movement comes from the few who join the procession, trailing behind Cairey, out of curiosity.

When the procession reaches the very end of the exposition room, the throne is turned around to face the maroon curtain. It's so far away now that when Cairey turns around he finds that he can block it out with the tip of his finger. The disciples form a wall before the throne & Simon's voice returns on the speaker.

"Line up if you'd like to meet HELEN! Don't be shy. She won't be going anywhere for a long time! Step right up!"

Cairey is the first in line. The wall of Symon's parts for him. He's ecastatic as he's strapped into the throne. His wrists are tied to its armrests. & the Symon that stands before him, readying the headpiece, pulls his mask aside. It's the real Simon. His eyes are blue. He winks at Cairey & lifts a finger to his lips. He covers his face with the mask again. Cairey feels the black crown descend onto his head. A countdown comes from the speakers & just before its end, he sees Ophelia amongst the onlookers, pointing directly at him. Then he feels an electric jolt course through his body & everything goes black.

He opens his eyes to find that he's still strapped into the throne. The exposition room is empty now. He's alone. He hears the sound of dripping water. He looks down at his feet & finds them submerged. The water line rises to his ankles & then past his calves. Soon, the throne lifts off the floor. It floats him down the rows of glass cubes. Inside he sees himself enacting every act of murder & suicide, repeating endlessly. The water level rises even more. By the time he reaches the entrance, every cube is submerged. Then, the water splits open before him. He descends rapidly down the fissure's incline. He passes through the maroon curtain, crashing through a pane of glass, & falls into an abyss. He cannot see anything. He feels his straps & the crown holding him to the throne as his body floats & air passes, whipping coldly through his clothes. The throne tilts forward until it's perpendicular. He faces the abyss he's falling into directly. Then there's another jolt. Something has grabbed the throne. He hears the crunch of its talons crushing holes in it behind his back. He hears a voice inside his head. He recognizes it, but cannot place its source.

"You've chosen how it ends," it says. Its voice is gravelled & slow. "But you've fallen once again. Though I warned you of this scheme, I never had much hope for you. I had to intervene."

The throne ceases its decline as the creature that's snagged it turns it upside down. Cairey hangs now, stunned. The sound of the falling breeze in the abyss is replaced with the sound of beating wings.

"If I had not caught you then you would have disappeared, exactly as you wanted, & precisely as I'd feared. He steals souls souls with his dark crowns, which then are lost in dreams. & once their drowned, he uses them to labor for his schemes. After all your years of drifting I could not allow this end. Do you recall the pact you made & promised to defend? Or did he steal that memory? I'll show you once again."

The throne descends slowly. Cairey makes out patches of light in the abyss below him. Moonlight reflects in it like water. Soon a figure appears against this dark sea. He sees himself as a child, rowing a canoe in the dark. He is wearing a dark crown. He asks "Tinfasel?"

"Yes" the creature says "that's one name that he has used, but he takes many forms. His spirit is diffused. You have met him many times. & You've refused his gifts, but other times excused them. The last was this abyss. He'd gotten you confused & you thought you could depose me. This is a common fantasy of those who haven't known me. I could have let you trade your soul. That was the end you craved, but Ends are under my control, & in this one you're saved."

They approach an island in the water. The creature lowers the throne to the ground. He reveals himself to Cairey. The feathers of his wings glow blue in the moonlight. His face is like a lion's. His talons are those of an eagle. His eyes are like opals & are larger than Cairey's head. He splays himself before the throne, reclining like an emperor on his triclinium.

"Is this a dream or is this real?" Cairey asks.

The creature laughs.

"It is exactly as it seems. Here nothing is concealed."

"Where am I?" Cairey asks "Where is here?"

The creature looks disappointed.

"You are on the furthest isle. Don't you recall Lake Lear?"

"I'm dreaming then" says Cairey "& you're HELEN then I guess."

The creature frowns.

"Oh Leaf. I must profess that you tempt me to regret saving you from your willful dance with death. I had thought you'd understand, but truly you are slow. I've given you another chance, but that's the last I owe."

The creature rises before the throne & inhales deeply. He exhales a blast of fire against it with a deafening roar. Cairey's restraints burn to ashes, but his body is unharmed.

"You are free now Leaf. Do anything you please. I've given you your ending back. You are herenow released."

The creature flies off into the starlit sky & Cairey is left on the scorched throne with his crown. He raises his arms before him. He inspects his hands. He rises from the throne & takes his first step onto the island. It is exactly as he'd remembered it from his dreams. He waits for something to happen, for a storm to come, for anything, but nothing changes for hours. He inspects every inch of the isle & finds the canoe tied to a tree at its edge. The inscription is there. "Lucremorn" he says.

He paddles it out into the lake, but no matter how long he paddles in any direction, he finds nothing but more water. The island remains at the edge of his horizon & ceases shrinking in his sight. Time passes. Or it seems to pass. But the stillness of this world renders it impossible for him to tell how long he spends doing anything. He paddles, refusing to look back for as long as his will holds out, but when he inevitably succumbs to his curiosity & looks over his shoulder, he finds he hasn't moved at all. The horizon in front of him is clouded with mist. There are no other shores to find. Centuries pass this way, perhaps eons. There is no way of knowing. He almost forgets that he's ever left the lake.

Eventually he looks at his reflection in the water. He's avoided this out of fear. He sees his face. He sees how old he's grown. His hair is grey. His face is wrinkled. He sees the crown. He inspects it so long that he feels disconnected from what stares back at him. Is this his face? He wonders. He reaches to the crown, intent on removing it, but as he touches it, he is overwhelmed with a sense of dread. He feels that if he removes it, he will disappear entirely. He watches his reflection again. He watches it as he reaches his hands to the crown, & as he touches it again, the reflection disappears. In its place, a circle opens in the water. Inside the circle he sees a white room. He tilts his head & the room move away. He sees figures in masks. He releases his grip on the crown & this vision disappears. He tries it again. The circle opens again. Inside it he sees a room full of blue balloons. He tries it again. The circle opens again. Inside it he sees a girl he doesn't recognize sitting at a desk. A blue pen hangs from her mouth. He tries it again. The circle opens again. He sees another girl. He thinks he recognizes her hair, but he cannot remember her name. He tries it again. The circle opens again. Inside it he sees nothing. He returns to his routines.

Eventually, he decides to remove the crown. Whenever he's tried to lift it a crippling pain surges through his body. The crown seems fused to his skull. It is impossibly heavy & the pain it discharges dissuades its removal. He's tried many times, but always gives up & returns to his routines. He paddles endlessly. He retreads the island. He swims & finds that he cannot drown. The water is infinitely deep. He returns to the surface. He returns to the canoe. He treads the island. He waits. He repeats himself. He exhausts every possibility. All that remains is the removal of the crown. The pain still dissaudes him. It is only once he suspects that he will die soon, once his reflection looks sickly & corpselike in the waters, that he decides to pull it off despite the pain. He paddles out, as far as he can & watches himself in his reflection. With his hands on the crown, a circle forms in the water. He sees himself in it. He is on his knees, spattered in blue paints. Jolts of electric pain shoot down his spine. He pulls through his agony. His eyes clamp shut.. His veins bulge. His feels like he is dying, but succeeds in wrenching it from his head.

He opens his eyes. He sees a face hovering over him.

"Cairey? Are you alright?"

It's one of the girls from the reflections. He cannot remember her name. He stares at her silently.

"You don't look to good. Are you alright? Here-"

She extends her arm to him. He takes it & lets himself be pulled from his throne. He looks around. He's in a large white room. People in masks are staring at him. He starts to remember.

"Where am I?" he asks her.

"Oh Cairey" she replies, "we're at the Museum, don't you remember? Do you remember me? Are you okay? What the fuck is going on with this? What did you do to him?"

She shouts at the camera crew.

"No. I don't. I don't remember anything. But wait. I think it's coming back to me. I sort of remember. I was on an island for a long time. There was a dragon. & a boat. Were you there? I saw you there I think. Is this real? Where's Simon?"

She looks horrified.

A voice booms through the room.

"What did you think of it Cairey? Was she everything you imagined?"

Cairey looks around at the crowd. A camera zooms into his face. A boom mic hovers over his head.

"I did not like it. I'd like to leave now."

The voice booms back: "What do you mean Cairey? Were you not entertained?"

Ophelia takes his hand & whispers: "I think we need to get you out of here Cairey. Are you okay? Do you need help? I don't like all of this. I don't know what to do."

Cairey relinquishes her hand. He says: "It's okay. I don't know either. I don't know who you are. I don't know any of you. But I think I have to go to the End now."

"What? Cairey, what are you talking about?" She looks concerned.

He feels something in his back pocket. He reaches his hand to it. He feels the coins. He starts to remember.

"I'm okay" he lies, "You should go on without me. All of this, whatever it is. I'm going to go now."

He leaves her behind. He feels drawn to the end of the hall. He passes through the curtain. He passes through tunnel & the gates. He passes through the corridor. & takes the elevator up. The voice in the elevator says: "Cairey? What are you doing? I told you there was no turning back! Have you forgotten your mission?"

"I don't know you & I'm leaving" he replies. He flips the coins in his back pocket with his fingers. They provide him a sense of stability. They are real tangible things.

He exits the elevator into the Exhibition room. It's still teeming with guests. He feels as if an eternity has passed since he had been there. He feels that his memories belong to someone else. Voices collide & echo against the towers of cubes. No one knows what's happened to him. Everything has continued in his absence. The thought makes him smile. He feels calm. His head feels light & clear. He leaves the Exhibition & follows signs for the exit. Glowing red arrows lead him. He pauses, remembering the Lobby. It seems a half-remembered dream. He follows the next red arrow, & there it is. He has found the Side Exit. &

just before leaving the Museum, coatless, to feel the miraculous rain falling like a blessing onto the infathomable street, he sees something on the wall to his right. He sees a painting hanging. It is a painting that he recognizes. It used to mean a lot to him, he recalls. It reminds him of his island. It reminds him of the relief he'd felt when he'd taken off the crown. This must be it, he thinks. This must be the ending. He sees a plaque beside the painting. It reads:

"Blue Skiddoo" by Cairey Turnbull

"This painting was created by Mr. Cairey Turnbull during his time at the General Arts Youniversity. It was the first part of a cycloroma he never finished. This painting was sold to the furniture retailer Flöskel & renamed "Blue Moon." It went onto sell hundreds of thousands of copies. It was one of the most popular paintings of the decade. Unfortunately, Mr. Turnbull received no royalties for his work. His mental collapse upon discovering this has been the subject of many dissertations. Most conclude that he had simply gone insane. He had believed the original painting to be entirely lost until he discovered that it was on display at the Museum of Expressive Humanism, right here, by the side exit. Upon discovering it, he pressed his hands against the painting. To his surprise, they sank into it. He pressed his arms into the painting. Then he pressed his shoulders & then his head into the painting. The painting swallowed him entirely. All of this was captured by our security cameras. Experts have analyzed the footage, but to this day, there is still no explanation for what became of him. The mystery remains."

INCONCLUSIVE FRAGMENT
...the nameless Knight in Lucremorn
grew weaker by the day.
His years passed slow as centuries.
His drifting never swayed.
His body aged from gold to grey.
His bones began to ache.
& still he floated all his life
reflecting on the lake.
So long therein he lay adrift,
his memories decayed.
He questioned if the Aphorapt
& Branche were but his dreams.
He wondered if the dragon's words
were really what they seemed
& if the journey of his life
was but a madness spell
& if his drift in Lucremorn
was his eternal Hell
but voices in the moonlit mists
would sing to him at night
instilling doubts or assuring him
his ending was in sight
or warning him of other men
who'd quit before the rain
& lost therein their recompense
for loneliness & pain.
He hears a voice sing to him now
as death creeps through his veins
as breathing becomes tiresome
& thinking's fully waned.
He shuts his eyes, convinced he's failed
& hears this distant song,
a melody he's long forgot
but still, he hums along,
& fading into death's beyond
he feels a kiss of flame
upon his weather-beaten flesh

which thaws his frozen veins
as over him a thundercloud
of fire starts to swarm
& all amassed its contents fall
in droplets red & warm
& ruby coins of substance strange
engraved with foreign runes
fall upon his shuttered eyes
& on his lips are strewn.
He awakes convinced he's died
& left the fallen earth.
Thus it's with incredulence
he greets his own rebirth.
A whirlpool in the water forms
& in it starlight glows
as bright as day's reflective beams
from mountaintops of snow.
& bearing forth the lake-locked star
is his abandoned muse.
She sings to him, "Oh Leaf, Poor Leaf,
what torments you've gone through.
The curse of Tinfasel has passed.
Our kingdom's now renewed.
Yet there are other realms to free
& We have more to do..."

Printed in Great Britain
by Amazon

11236274R00098